DAUGHTER OF HADES

ENDANGERED

BOOK ONE

FoxTales Press

DANI HOOTS

Endangered
Daughter of Hades, #1
Second Edition
© 2020 FoxTales Press
Content and line edits by Justin Boyer of
Bibliophile's Workshop
Cover Design Copyright © 2020 by Biserka Designs
All rights reserved.

No part of this publication may be reproduced, distributed, or transmitted in any form or by any means, or stored in a database or retrieval system without the prior written permission of the author.

This is a work of fiction. All characters and events portrayed in this novel are fictitious and are products of the author's imagination. Any resemblance to actual events, locales, or persons, living or dead, is entirely coincidental.

ISBN for paperback: 978-1-942023-40-1

ISBN for ebook: 978-1-942023-41-8

Chapter 1

Chrys

Hello and welcome to the Underworld. My name is Chrys, and I am the daughter of Hades. May I take your coat?

I really wanted to say that to the group of recently deceased that stepped up to my father, begging him not to send them to Tartarus, the place of eternal torment—pretty much where all the bad people went. Beside Father was Minos, Rhadamanthys, and Aiakos, the other judges of the dead. I sure as Cronus didn't want to be judged by that deadly trio.

First off, they had been here longer than I had, since Zeus appointed them, and although nothing really ages here after death, they seemed to be older and grumpier than ever before. And I, unfortunately, had to witness today's session of pleas because "I needed to learn the ins and outs of the business in case anything ever happened." At least, that is what my father, Hades, kept telling me.

Father sat there, quiet, as the three stooges (that's what I called them in my head, if they ever found out, I would be in so much trouble) examined the next contestant. The man before them was on the fence of being sent to either Tartarus or the Asphodel Meadows, which was why he was being judged. I already knew my father's decision, since he was quite predictable when it came to judging people.

It would be Tartarus.

Father always took a long while, as if his decision hadn't already been made. He could have finished judging today's deceased already if he didn't take his time about it. It annoyed me tremendously, which I knew he could tell as I sat there nervously fighting with my dress sleeves.

One of the men went down on his knees. "Please, have mercy on me. I never meant to do those things, had I known— "

"Had you known, you would have been perfect, right?" Hades interrupted with a scowl. "Done everything you could to be in paradise? There are no second chances here, the gods have given humans a chance to obey them, a chance to live in paradise. It is not our fault you don't see the signs."

I let out a brief yawn, trying to cover it with my hand, but my father noticed right away and gave me one of his cold looks. I tried my hardest to sit up straight, to appear as though my mind hadn't drifted off to thinking about meeting up with my friends Huntley and A.J., or what I told Father was "being tutored about modern Earth affairs" by these friends of mine. Really, we just hung out and tried not to get into trouble.

Tried was the key word there.

"Tartarus. Send in the next one," Hades ordered.

Loud barking echoed through the throne room. I smiled as Cerberus came galloping towards the dead human. He screamed in terror as everyone did when greeting Cerberus. No one saw how clumsy this puppy really was, but thought it as one of the most terrifying beasts in all the Underworld. But I guess if he was taking me to my horrible fate, I would fear him too.

Nah, he's not scary. He's adorable.

The man screamed again as all three jaws bit at his clothes, dragging him out the door and down the chute that would send him to Tartarus. His soul would circle there in the deepest part of nothing for all of eternity.

Yawn. When would this be over?

I knew nothing else besides this life, as I have never traveled to any of the other worlds. A big complicated mess, but irritating nonetheless. Which led to why my friends and I got into just a bit of trouble every once in a while. But only in the Underworld, mind you. We couldn't ever leave.

My father judged different humans, demigods,

and creatures for another hour. I tried not to let my stomach grumble, as that wasn't something the goddess of the Underworld should never let happen. I wasn't to show any weakness, I wasn't to show anything less than divine perfection.

Well, at least Mother wasn't back yet to make matters worse.

Cerberus dragged away his last victim for the day while Father clapped his hands together. "Well that wraps up today. The three of you are dismissed. Chrys, come with me."

I felt as if my heart stopped, which would have been pointless even if it did because I was already in the world of the dead. So dying wouldn't get me out of the conversation I was dreading—the conversation of how I would eventually become goddess of all this. Boy, was I looking forward to that day.

It was way too much responsibility if you asked me. I just wanted to be a normal teen, even though I had been a teen for quite some time. The years passed by differently for the gods, something humans could never understand. And since I never really got to do what most teens did in any other world, I felt like I would never grow up and learn about the rest of the universe. I just wanted to explore, be able to go out into the worlds.

To be known.

"Yes, Father." I followed after him as he headed towards the hallway. Knowing Father, he was going to the patio that looked out at his entire world for a "talk." He was so predictable, especially after all this time. When you have Hades as your father, and he was the only constant in your life, you're bound to know him more than you want to, and spend more time than needed in the drab Underworld.

I was a few steps behind him, watching as he had his hands folded neatly behind himself, his short hair nicely trimmed, a new style the mortals were sporting. I didn't blame him for wanting to try to fit in with those that had recently died. That way they felt more at home. Except those who went to Tartarus. He didn't really care to fit in with those souls.

Cerberus sat in his corner of the hallway, next to the patio door, gnawing on three bones that I had given him the other day, ones discarded in the River Acheron. Father bent down and patted Cerberus on one of his heads. "You did good today. You deserve something a little special."

With a snap of his fingers, a large bone appeared in front of the puppy. All of his eyes widened, and each head howled a thank you before biting down on the new bone. I tried not to appear frustrated as it had taken me weeks to find the bone I had already given him. But it didn't matter, Cerberus looked so happy as all three of his heads tried to snap at each other, wanting the bone to itself.

I stepped outside with my father, looking upon all the Underworld from the patio. The dark sparkling water of Oceanus made up all the sky, and beyond that laid the human world, Earth. I had never seen yet, but one day wanted to. It was where all the deceased came from, a place that I only learned about in books and from tutors. Coming down in the middle of the clouds was the waterfall of

Phlegethon, souls in a blue fire all destined for Tartarus, the enormous gaping hole that didn't seem to ever have an end. They were all the wicked souls, the souls that had no chance at redemption. If I listened closely, I could hear their cries for help. Then again, that could have been the River Cocytus. It sounded like the wind, or at least that was what Huntley said, I wouldn't know.

Next, around River Phlegethon, was the palace itself. This was where I lived and spent most of my time. Since we had visitors every once in a while, Father was hesitant to even let me venture outside the palace. The palace was big, of course, as it held many of those who were more like guests than the deceased, although some weren't dead, like Hermes for example. How he got into the Underworld, Father could never figure out. It pissed him off every time Hermes showed up with a smirk on his face. Many beings were sent to search for the loophole that Hermes had found, but none figured it out. I always had to be cautious, though, as Hermes couldn't know I existed, especially since he was a kiss-up to Zeus, at least according to Father.

A lot of the others had been my tutors over the years, ranging from teaching me languages, history, culture, math, etc. I never understood why I needed to know these things, specifically since I never got to leave this realm.

The palace itself looked like something out of *Van Helsing*. One of my tutors called it 'a late gothic German style architecture like that of Eltz Castle'. Huntley said, 'holy fuck, it's Dracula's castle!'. I liked his description better. Also, calling it Dracula's castle made it easier to spook him with.

I loved it here and I could even watch some human movies in the Underworld. It was confusing though, as none were consistent with each other. I never could tell fact from fiction either, especially since those on Earth say the Underworld is a fictitious place. I loved seeing their faces when they found out the truth.

Beyond my home were the Elysian Fields and the Asphodel Meadows, where the good souls along with okay souls went. The Elysian Fields were nice, but I preferred the palace. And I wouldn't know what Tartarus was like because no one ever came back from there, at least not very often.

I stepped up to the railing next to Father. He wore his normal all-black suit and tie. Don't get me wrong, he looked good in black, but sometimes I just wished for a little more color. I was wearing an all-black dress, so I couldn't really talk. Then again, I only wore it because he insisted on it during the judging.

Also, my father wasn't bad looking. He had a chiseled jaw, high cheekbones, and good teeth. I mean, I wouldn't really know if he was good or bad looking, but that was what the maids said. Many of them didn't think my mother deserved such a beautiful god, as she was gone from this place nine months of the year, not to mention she snuck countless men in here during the three months she was here. Most of the workers called her a whore, and I didn't bother to blame or correct them.

"Why do you even have those sessions?" I decided I would be the first to talk. I hated it when we just stood there in silence. "You always sentence them to Tartarus."

He smiled, as if my question was comical. He wasn't as bad as people made him out to be. He was quite kind actually, and it wasn't his fault that Zeus sentenced him to rule over this part of the world. Although, when given the circumstances, he could turn dark in just a blink of an eye and show absolutely no mercy.

Which was why I never got on his bad side. At least, not completely.

"You know it's not that simple, my precious flower. There are some that are judged that do, in fact, deserve some sort of paradise instead of eternal torment. I can't let them get wrongly judged. You understand that, don't you?"

I let out a brief sigh. I understood, as we had gone over this many times before. I just hated sitting there, watching those stooges be idiots. I wondered whether I could pick new judges when Father passed on his legacy to me. Probably not since Zeus appointed them himself, and they were Zeus' sons, as were a good chunk of souls down here, and if I fired them, then Zeus would find out and I would be screwed.

Because I was never supposed to be born.

"I know," I mumbled.

He wrapped his arm around my shoulder and kissed my forehead. "Your mother will be coming home tonight. Are you excited?"

I tried not to roll my eyes, I truly did, but yeah, I rolled my eyes. Hard. Yes, I loved my mother, for the most part, and yes, I knew she cared for me in her own little way. But after having to deal with her drama for hundreds of years, I was getting sick of her.

Hades seemed disappointed with my lack of enthusiasm. "What's that look for? Don't you miss her?"

I looked up at the souls that came raining down into the Underworld and toward their destination through the River Acheron. "It's just hard to miss someone who, while here, only talks about Earth, all the things she sees and buys. She'd rather be part of that world than this one, even when the two of us are here. It doesn't make me feel like she wants to be with me."

"Your mother cares a lot about you, she's just bad at expressing it."

"And what about you? Do you really think she cares about you?" It was a harsh thing of me to ask, but it was also harsh of him to give her the benefit of the doubt.

"She does... in her own way."

I couldn't believe he was defending her after all these years. "She leaves for nine months of the year, Father. *Nine months.* In those nine months, you know she's sleeping with other men. Along with that, while she is here, she *sneaks* men in and has affairs with them. You know how many men of hers I have run into over the years? She doesn't want to be here anymore than I do—" I covered my mouth. I didn't mean to say that, it just slipped out.

Hades looked at me, his eyes alert, waiting to see if I would say anything else. His body seemed tight, reacting to the words I had let out by accident.

"You... you don't like it here either?"

"No, I do. This is your world, Father, everything you have built. I would want nothing else. Except..." I began, trying to find the right words. "I would like to see the Earth, or Olympus. I want to know what else is out there. I just learn about them from tutors, but I would like to experience it for myself. See the ocean, the sky... It's my dream."

He studied me closely. "You know that isn't possible, you know if you leave this place you will no longer be under my protection. The gods could hurt you, they will find out you exist and they will take you away from me."

I gave him one of my 'don't worry, I won't do anything stupid' smiles. "I know. I didn't say I would leave. I'm just saying that hopefully someday I can."

"So you won't leave me like everyone else?" For the first time, I saw the sadness in his eyes, the loneliness that came with his title being brought to the surface. It was why he didn't care what Persephone did behind his back, why he was willing to put up with it for the short time they had together during the year.

Why he cared for me so much and why he hid me from the other gods.

"No, never. I love you Father, nothing will ever change that."

He wrapped his arms around me. "The other reason I could never be mad at your mother is because she gave me the best thing I could ever ask for. My little flower in this dark world." He stepped back and smiled as he moved a piece of hair out of my face. "Now you better get going or you will be late for your tutoring lesson."

I smiled and nodded, hurrying off before he questioned what we would be tutoring, making me lie yet again. He couldn't, no he would never know, that Huntley and I would be playing some soccer instead of learning current earthly events.

But soccer was current, right? Yeah, I would keep telling myself that, otherwise I fear I would lose my mind being stuck here.

Chapter 2

Huntley

I kicked the soccer ball towards A.J.; Chrys still wasn't here yet, typical for her. You would think being the daughter of the Dark Lord of the Underworld that she would be on time every once in a while. But nope. Never. So instead I was stuck passing the ball back and forth with A.J., a blond, pretty boy that had lived over four thousand years ago as the King of Tyre, son of Poseidon, or something like that. He kept telling me about how great a king he was, but I always tuned him out. I honestly didn't care. I was a little sick of all these "sons of such-and-such god" who boast about their heroic tales while I, a mere human, would 'never understand'.

They got that right.

A.J. and I, what one could say, didn't get along very well. He saw me as a pipsqueak, someone who wasn't worth his time. Although humans and demigods coexisted in some areas of the Underworld, a lot didn't get along. At least that's what Chrys explained to me when I first came here. A.J. and I were prime examples of that. But we both wanted to be friends with Chrys, so when she was around, we kept our cool. Or, at least, we tried our best to keep our cool.

We didn't speak a word as we kicked the ball back and forth. As more time passed, the ball seemed to be going faster and faster, as each of us were kicking it harder and harder at each other. Suddenly the ball jumped up and hit me straight in the face.

"Oh, sorry. My bad," A.J. said a bit too flat toned.

I wanted to punch him. I wanted to punch him *so*

badly. He was just like the jocks in my old school, the ones who had made my life a living nightmare. Well, in reality A.J. wasn't *as* bad as them. Not to mention that living in the Palace of Hades was better than my life before I died. Before—

Chrys stepped in, stopping me from deciding to kick the ball straight at A.J.'s stomach. She always showed up at the most inopportune times, but I was glad to see her nevertheless. I knew that sitting next to her father, Hades, the God of the Underworld, always made her tired and in the need for some relaxation. Which was why, as her "tutor", we were "learning" soccer. Really, we were just goofing off. But for some reason, instead of just being the two of us, A.J. had joined us. Again. Seriously, this guy needed to take a hint. Chrys wasn't interested in him, yet he always joined us in games and hanging out. Maybe he did just want to be her friend. She was a goddess after all.

Chrys still wore her lacy black dress, one that left me only to imagine what she would look like in just black lace. I tried my hardest not to think about it, but damn she was beautiful. Her long chestnut hair was still in curls and she examined us with her dark eyes. "You two behaving yourselves?"

We both nodded in unison. "Yeah."

She snapped her fingers and her dress morphed into grey sweats and a pink tank-top. I tried to avert my eyes when she did stuff like that because I couldn't keep away some of the thoughts that ran through my mind.

Oh yeah, did I mention she was Hades' daughter? Yeah, that was always a buzzkill.

I couldn't imagine what he would do to me if I ever laid a hand on his daughter, with her permission of course. I would say he would kill me, but I was already dead. So whatever he would do to me had to be much, much worse.

Chrys kicked the ball up into her hands. "So, are we playing one-on-one-on-one?"

A.J. and I glanced at each other and shrugged.

"Sure, whatever you want," I said as I straightened out my black sleeveless shirt. She sort of nodded, but didn't let go of the ball.

A.J. stared at her a little longer. "What's wrong? Did something happen?"

I hated it when he noticed things like that, made me look like I hadn't a clue. I knew that they had been together for a very long time (again, as friends) so they learned a lot about each other during that time.

She frowned as she twirled the ball in her hands. "Mother's coming home today."

Was it already that time of year? It was hard to tell when the Underworld didn't have seasons. For that reason, I neglected even keeping track of what day it was because, well, it wasn't like I had anything else to do for the rest of eternity.

As for Chrys' mother, Persephone... she was an interesting woman. She was kind of like those moms you knew were sleeping with the pool guy, but the husbands didn't care. Actually, it was exactly like that as Persephone snuck men in all the time. In front of Hades. In front of her own daughter. Then apparently when Hades tried to sleep with a nymph named Minthe, Persephone trampled her and she became mint. I still didn't know if I believed that, even after being in the Underworld and hanging out with gods and all. Though Chrys told me other stories about gods, that made this one seem more plausible. The gods were up to some weird shit, I tell you.

So one could see why Chrys got upset when her mother was back for the three months of the year. They didn't exactly get along.

Although Persephone did try what she considered "hard" and you could tell she loved her daughter even if it felt forced, she never really took the time to understand Chrys and I think that was why Chrys never looked forward to her mother being home. That is, at least not since I've known her.

I never looked forward to family time when I was alive either, so I could relate.

"We can do something else if you want—play some video games or something," I said. Yes, we had video games down here. It was great. I also had some contraband that was burning a hole in my pocket, but couldn't bring it up with A.J. there. He would simply disapprove.

She shook her head. "No, I think some physical activity would be good for me. I need to get my mind off it all." Dropping the ball, she kicked it over to me. "So let's play."

We played for what seemed like hours, and it probably was. Time always went by fast, yet didn't seem to move at all since we were kind of stuck here. I couldn't wait until the day came when I had been here for millennia and I'm just like oh, has it been that long already?

And I would still suck at soccer.

I was losing big time, and Chrys was winning. I didn't know if A.J. was letting her win or if she was just having a good day in general. Maybe it had something to do with letting stress off about her mom's upcoming visit. It was usually tied between those two, both were part god after all, or fully goddess in her case.

Chrys had collapsed in the middle of the gym, acting as if she had died from exhaustion, yet laughing hysterically as A.J. frowned, looking quite sad that she had gotten the ball past us and into the goal.

I patted A.J. on the back. "Tough luck."

He glared at me. "Touch me again, you're dead."

I lifted my hand off of him and went to help Chrys up. I lent her a hand and as she grabbed it, instead of letting me help her up, of course, she pulled me over her back and I hit the gym floor with a loud bang. That was definitely going to leave a mark. She busted up laughing again.

"I can't believe you fell for that gag again." She rolled over to face me. I didn't feel like getting up, as my body was in a lot of pain.

Yup, one could feel pain in the Underworld. It was great... Though it would pass soon, it was still inconvenient. But at least I lost to Chrys and damn she smelled good, even after playing for a couple of hours. She smelled like a sweet flower.

"Hey," I said as I groaned. "If you are going to be like that, maybe I won't share with you what I have in my pocket."

Her eyes widened, and then her lips turned into a smile. "You didn't."

I pulled out a small plastic bag full of little red seeds. They were better than any drug I had ever had on Earth, and believe me I had tried a few. "Just you and me. Our little secret."

She glanced over at A.J. who was kicking the goal post, still pissed off that Chrys had bested him. He never ate anything, I swore. Chrys had asked him once to join us and he chewed the both of us out and stormed off. Apparently they were some forbidden fruit of the gods, and anyone who ate them would have to face the wrath of Hades. We didn't see A.J. for a couple of days. It was awesome. But nevertheless, he came back, and we never brought it up to him again. Kept it our little secret. Because, seriously, there was no way Hades would ever find out.

Biting her lip, she nodded. "Yeah, let's ditch him and go to my room."

I smiled. I wished she wasn't talking about just eating the seeds, but that day probably wouldn't come anytime soon. "Your turn to come up with a lie."

She rolled her eyes as she stood up. It really was her turn, as I had made up the lie of "Hades wanted me to teach her about modern politics. You interested in joining us?" What I had learned over the couple of years here was that A.J. hated learning about modern governments. He couldn't get over the fact that he was once King of Tyre, and the fact that no one I knew had ever heard of the place pissed him off a lot.

"Follow my lead," she whispered to me, then turned to A.J. "Hey, I'm getting a bit tired and I need to get ready for dinner with my mother tonight. Call it good?"

If I watched A.J.'s expression closely, it always amazed me how he could give me such a disgusted look, yet look at Chrys with such kindness at the same time. He was talented indeed.

"Of course, Chrys. Go get some rest. Then tomorrow I shall have my revenge on the court," A.J. kissed her hand and watched as she left. Then he turned to me with a frown. "You two are going to go eat that fruit, aren't you?"

I froze. I had no idea how he knew we still did that. "What are you talking about?"

That was a stupid thing to say to a demigod. Do you know how strong demigods are? Very. The answer is *very*.

A.J. had me pinned to the wall, his hand around my throat. "Are you an idiot?" he snarled. "The fruit is called 'forbidden' for a reason. Only Hades is allowed to eat that fruit. If he finds out his daughter has been eating it with a *human*, he will be pissed. Do you know what happens when Hades is pissed?"

"Bad things?" I choked.

"Very bad things. And guess what? He will take his anger out on the both of us. I don't want any part of that, do you hear me? If you two get caught, you better leave me out of it." His crystal blue eyes stared at me full of fury. I struggled to nod.

"Yeah, don't worry, I will tell him it's my fault. Don't worry about it."

He let go of my throat, but jabbed his finger into my collarbone. "I shouldn't have let Chrys save you. I should have let Charon find you and dispose of you like all the rest."

I stared at him, dumbfounded. "What are you talking about?"

Instead of answering my question, A.J. shook his head and left me standing there. I sighed. Neither he nor Chrys ever told me how I ended up in this palace. She said it was because she needed a modern tutor, someone who could tell her about what the Earth was like. Yeah, I was pretty sure there were many more qualified than I was, but I didn't complain. I saw the alternatives and since I wasn't sure as to which of the three afterlives I would go to (well, which of the two to be honest), I decided being Chrys' tutor wasn't a bad choice after all, not to mention it meant I got to work closely with the most beautiful woman in all the worlds. I didn't care that I hadn't met any other goddesses, other than Persephone. And I had to admit I thought she was quite beautiful when I first saw her.

That was the day I taught Chrys what a MILF was, so I guess I was a tutor of modern affairs, just not ones that she really needed to learn. Teaching Earth slang wasn't really furthering her education, at least with respects to what goddesses of the underworld needed to know.

As I walked down the hallway towards Chrys' room, I passed Hades' office. I could hear him playing the song "Way Down Hadestown". He really liked that song. It was quite entertaining, though Chrys didn't seem to think so. She was quite annoyed by it honestly, but I presume she has heard her father playing it a lot more than I had. It seemed like a tune that foreshadowed the appearance of Chrys' mother. It must have been their song, so to speak. Persephone probably hated it, if we were honest. It was about going down into the Underworld, or at least that part of New Orleans the song described. Very ironic, if you ask me.

Hades must have heard me in the hallway because just as I passed by, he stepped out.

"Huntley, have you and my daughter finished

your tutoring for the day?" Hades asked.

My heart feeling as if it were going to jump right out of my chest. Cool part is that I would still go on being "alive" here if that happened. It would hurt, but hey, it would make for a nice story to tell others for eternity. I turned, and there in front of me stood the Lord of Darkness, Death himself.

He wasn't how I pictured him. In fact, I laughed when I first saw him because I thought someone was playing some kind of joke. There was no joke, he was indeed Hades and even though Chrys elbowed me to shut up about the fact he didn't look scary at all, I had to learn my lesson the hard way. He was indeed scary when he wanted to be, and ever since then he hadn't liked me. Not sure if it was because of that incident or because I spent a lot of time with his daughter, but either way he liked glaring daggers at me for no reason.

But seriously, this man was sexy, even I would admit that. He would make a great movie villain, honestly. He had black hair, was clean-shaven, and was always wearing a dark suit. That wasn't how I pictured the dark lord to be. He was supposed to be scary, you know, with horns and goat legs (apparently that was Pan), I don't know. Not *sexy*.

But that didn't mean he wasn't vicious by any means. I had seen him get angry and A.J. was right, I never wanted to be on his bad side. Which was why I made sure I would never get caught. And why I wouldn't ever lay a hand on his daughter either. He made that clear the first time we met, when Chrys begged him to let me be her tutor.

"No, we still need to go over some new geography. She keeps messing up her Nordic cities. Can't blame her, they have some really weird names," I lied to the God of the Underworld. I would say I was going to go to hell for that, but...

He inspected me, his eyes narrowing, and nodded. "I see. Well, her mother will be home in a few hours. See to it that she is ready and *on time*. She has a problem with tardiness, as you know."

So he even knew that. Surprise, surprise. "Yes, sir."

"Carry on then. and thank you for training my daughter so well," he said without a hint of actual thankfulness. I wasn't sure if he was being sarcastic or if he just felt like it needed to be said, even though he still hadn't quite decided if he liked me or not.

"No problem, have fun doing... whatever you are doing." And as quickly as I could, I got out of being in his intimidating presence. I didn't like being around him for more than a little amount of time by myself. I just knew I was going to say something stupid out of sheer nervousness.

I could feel his eyes on me until I rounded the corner. I let out the breath I had been holding and then knocked on Chrys' door. She opened it.

"Get in before I have to hear that stupid song of his any longer." She grabbed me by the shirt and pulled me inside.

"Whoa, someone's addicted to this stuff." I watched as she locked the door behind her. She was wearing jeans, converse, and a long black shirt. Her hair was pinned up, which I always thought looked best on her. I glanced around the room. Dark purple and black were the theme of her room. Curtains, pillowcases, lampshades, comforter. It was all the same. I knew with a snap of her fingers should could make it all a shade of pink that would make me vomit.

The walls were decorated with metal and alternative rock posters. She had Oomph!, Rammstein, Amaranthe, Nightwish, Before Their Eyes, Escape the Fate, and that was just to name a few. I got her hooked on metal. It was great.

"No, it's just if I hear that song one more time I am going to go to my father's office and break all his CDs. At least until he learns about MP3s." She let out a brief sigh, as if even the thought of the song left her exhausted. "He thinks it's hilarious because it's about him. He plays it mostly before Mother is back because she won't let him play it while she's around. Anyway, I need some *good* music. What should we listen to?"

I shrugged. I really didn't have a preference. "Up to you. Your room."

She smiled as she pressed a button on her stereo. "Oomph! it is."

The song lyrics started to play. *"Oh my time is up, I know you're gonna burn me. Your judgement's coiled just like a snake around my neck."*

I pulled out the bag of a couple of red seeds. Okay, so they were pomegranate seeds, but damn these weren't like any pomegranates I had ever had. These things could give a person a high without any of the side effects. It was great. Just one seed was all you needed.

Chrys looked as if she couldn't hold back her anticipation. She sat across from me in her black bean bag chair (I know, right? I have corrupted this poor goddess) biting her lip and playing with her nails. I opened up the bag and grabbed one to put in her hand.

"I can't wait to forget about Mother coming home. I'm so sick of her already, and she's not even here yet."

"Won't make the problem go away though." I was one to talk, that was the exact reason I was *here*.

She looked a little sad as she paused to take the seed. "Yeah, well, a brief escape from time-to-time is enough. Anyway, where did you get them this time?" she asked as she stared at the seed in her hand.

I shrugged. "Just been grabbing one at a time for a while now. No one notices when I only grab one. Your father has them stashed in quite a few places all over his domain."

Chrys shook her head. "I can't imagine him ever taking these. He's too strict. I bet they are my mother's. I'm surprised I have never seen her high on these before." She popped the morsel in her mouth and laid back in the beanbag chair. "These are heavenly. I'm so glad we found them."

The song kept playing. *"Oh my time is up, and Heaven's gates are bolted. But now I'm not even sure if they want me down in Hell."*

I grabbed the remaining one and put it in my mouth. Instantly I felt like I was floating on clouds. The room felt as if it were spinning, yet not in a way that made one sick. It was like a surreal dream, as colors erupted around me.

Yet even with all of this, I couldn't get what A.J.

had said out of my head.

Chapter 3

Chrys

Mother was home.

I forced myself to smile but, damn, I didn't want to. She was the same mother who left me behind for most of the year; the one who didn't care that it was just me and Father in the Underworld. Sure I had Huntley and A.J. but it wasn't the same as having one's own mother home with them for more than just a few weeks each year.

Although I wanted her home and for us to all be a family, I couldn't stand her being so fake, acting as if she missed this place even a tad. She didn't want to be here—she wanted to be back on Earth or in Olympus with her mother Demeter. The only reason she was in the Underworld was because of some deal she made with Hades.

Yay for gods making things difficult for themselves and everyone everywhere.

"My precious flower." Persephone wrapped her arms around me, her hands still full of shopping bags. She always brought back earthly outfits. I didn't quite understand why, as she had so many clothes already. "I missed you so much."

"I missed you too, Mother."

I must have not seemed very enthusiastic as she backed away far enough to make eye contact. Well, kind of. She was wearing huge shades, making it hard to see her eyes. "What's wrong? Didn't you miss me?"

I smiled a little more convincingly. "Of course I did. I'm just tired, we played a lot of soccer today."

She bit her lip. "With *Huntley*?"

Great. this conversation again. "Yes with

Huntley."

"Have you two done *the deed* yet?"

I felt my blood start to heat up. Every time he came up in conversation it turned to sex. She didn't understand what it was like to just be friends with men.

Before I could say anything, Father appeared next to me. "The boy is still here, isn't he? You know I would never let that *human* touch my daughter."

Persephone took off her shades so she could roll her amber eyes at him. "Here we go again. How do you expect her to ever grow up if her father's a constant overprotective prude?"

He folded his hands behind his back calmly. He always kept his cool around Mother, somehow. "I just want what's best for my daughter."

I watched as Mother and Father just stared at each other, the air becoming cold around them. You would think when a husband and wife were gone for long periods of time that they would embrace or kiss or something. Not these two. Things were always so awkward or aggressive between them.

"Well Huntley is just my mentor," I interjected. "He's teaching me all about the world."

Mother turned back to me with a smile. "Right. Of course, he must be very knowledgeable. All boys at that age are." There was almost a hint of sarcasm in her voice, but I ignored it. "What about A.J. then, hmm? You've known him for quite some time."

"Like my daughter would ever fall for a son of Poseidon," Hades retorted sharply.

Persephone turned back to him, and they looked as if they were about to start another argument. So I naturally intervened. "No boys right now. If I ever do fall in love with someone, you two would be the first to know. Okay? Now, let's go have something to eat, I'm starving."

Really, I wasn't that hungry, but I wanted this awkward conversation to end. Hades smiled softly, gesturing towards the door for the both of us. I knew he had been planning this dinner for quite some time, picking the best food in all the worlds.

But interestingly enough, he never had pomegranates.

How Huntley and I came across those seeds was such a strange happenstance. We had snuck into Father's office one day, just out of curiosity really, and in the bottom drawer there were hundreds of these things. So, naturally, we took a few. Huntley had said they looked like pomegranate seeds on Earth, but he had never had one that gave him that effect. They were like drinking gold, giving us a high that felt like nothing I had ever experienced before. When we showed them to A.J. however, he got mad at us, calling them the forbidden fruit of the Underworld. I didn't see him for a couple of days and I had no idea as to where he went. Then he came back and acted like it never happened, which was exactly why I never mentioned it to him again.

I always thought about asking my father about the seeds, but since they were hidden in and locked in his desk, and we had a couple before I thought about asking, I decided him finding out now wouldn't be the best idea. Although he was a kind and great father, he could be terrifying and would send Huntley to Tartarus without a second thought, since he would automatically blame him. So I kept my mouth shut about it, though Huntley seemed to find some every once in a while. I didn't ask how and he didn't tell because if Father found out, I didn't want to be able to tell him what Huntley did. It was the only way I could keep him safe.

So far so good though, as Huntley hadn't been caught and Father didn't suspect a thing. I wondered what would be worse to him, finding out that we had a relationship or that we had been eating this forbidden fruit... Probably about the same I would think.

As for being in a relationship, there was no way I'd get into one. I saw what destruction love brought to the gods, I saw how much it hurt my father, an eternity of being with someone who changed their mind. I couldn't do that, especially not to Huntley. I knew he was dead, that he really had nowhere else to go. But to have to be with me for that long, I couldn't ever imagine making him do that. He didn't understand what it was like to be alive for such a long time. He had only been here for a few years. He had no idea.

A.J., on the other hand, had been here for four thousand years. He knew the complications it brought, being with someone for an eternity. He had the opportunity to go to Elysium, but he decided to stay in the palace for now. Whenever he did decide to leave, he wouldn't be able to come back to the palace, as no souls could move among the different realms of the dead once they left the palace. Why he decided to stay around, I wasn't quite sure. It wasn't because of me though, I knew that. Especially after that one night we had a little too much wine, and we came close to doing things I would have regretted, but he insisted we stop. He never brought it up again, and I tried to forget it had ever happened.

Anyway, Father went overboard as he usually did with food preparation. There were only three of us and yet we had a long table full of food. It all smelled fantastic as different waves of scents floated around us. Sweet, savory, everything cooked, or chilled, to the perfect temperature. He had overdone it yet again. I knew that after we were done that the three stooges along with A.J. and Huntley could take their share, so it didn't go to waste. But it was still ridiculous.

Hades pulled out the chair for Persephone and I. We both took our seats across from each other and Father sat at the head of the table. Our gold glasses were already full of red wine. I took a sip. Tasted perfect as usual.

"Eat whatever your heart desires, I've been saving all of this for tonight." Hades smiled. "Bon appétit."

"Compensating for something, Hades?" Persephone snapped her napkin to unfold it and placed it on her lap. "Do you think you are really impressing anyone?"

I rolled my eyes. Not this again. Seriously, every time she came home and Father had a big dinner prepared, she had to make snide comments. Then the one time he had nothing planned, she threw a fuss.

"I just want the best for my two favorite women. Do I have to have any other reason?" Hades asked as he took a bite of his salad.

"Why is *Minthe* here?"

Here we go. It always came back to that.

"You know I regret ever falling for her. Please, can we just have a peaceful dinner? How was Earth? Did you and Demeter do anything special?" Hades asked, trying to change the subject. *Smooth, Father.*

Mother looked like she wanted to argue some more, but resisted the urge as I was still sitting there, twirling my linguine nervously. "We saw some plays. We spent a lot of time in London this year. So much great food and shopping."

I coughed. "And men."

Persephone didn't seem to notice my comment, but Father gave me a look to stop talking. Hades turned back to her. "That sounds lovely."

"And what about you, flower, how was your time here?" she directed her question towards me.

I kept twirling my linguine around and around with my fork. "Fine. Normal. Helped judge people with Father. Huntley has been teaching me some geography. Today we focused on Asian cities."

"Really?" Hades took a bite of his kale. "When I ran into him earlier, he said you were studying Nordic cities."

Shit. Huntley should have told me he ran into him. "Yeah, Nordic cities are in Asia aren't they?" I tried to act dumb. I knew the difference.

Hades shook his head. "No, they aren't."

"Oh, crap. Looks like I'll need to study some more."

"Mm." Father stared at me with suspicious eyes. He could always see past my lies, which was why I usually hid the truth instead of flat out lying.

"Father says I'm getting good at judging." I tried to change the subject back to earlier today. Like father, like daughter. "If I pay more attention, he might even let me decide some fates."

"And if you start showing up on time instead of always being late," he commented.

Persephone smiled. "She takes after me in that regard. Good to know she takes after some of my traits and annoys you with them."

Family dinners were always the best.

Cerberus whimpered from underneath the table. I grabbed one of the steaks from a platter in front of me and threw it down to the ground. I was hoping Mother wouldn't notice, but she did.

"Cerberus! Out!"

The dog whimpered some more as he grabbed his treat and scurried off.

Mother scowled. "I hate that creature. I don't know why you keep it here, Hades, as if this place isn't horrid enough already."

"Three months is all I ask, Persephone. Stop acting like it's torture," Hades commented.

Mother slammed her fork down. "Torture? I wish it was torture. I'm in Hell, Hades, literally in Hell. This is not the life I chose, I can't stand it here. There is nothing worth my time here!"

She said that in front of me. In front of her daughter, who was forbidden to step foot out of the Underworld. Who was never allowed to know anything else, according to Father. The only way she could see me was if she came here and apparently I wasn't worth it to her.

I stood up. "Excuse me, Father. I'm not that hungry."

Hades was about to say something, but he waved me off with permission to leave. I turned and walked out of the dining hall, but not before I heard them start arguing again.

Tears fell from my eyes as I hurried to my room. I just wanted to curl up on my bed and listen to music, let all the pain just fade away with the beats of the song. It's the only way I learned how to cope with the pain in my chest and not let it explode out in blind rage, as that never ended well for anything around me. It was something Huntley had taught me, and I was glad too since one time he almost ended up on the wrong side of my rage. It wasn't fair to have all this power and be expected to have a control of it at all times. I had no idea how Father did it.

Huntley had helped a lot since he came here only a couple of years ago. He was kinder than he would like to admit, and always helped me when I needed him. And he did actually teach me a lot about the world called Earth that I didn't know, it just wasn't necessarily stuff my father wanted me learning about.

Speaking of Huntley, he was in the hallway as I turned around the corner. I hated it when he saw me like this—showing any kind of weakness. It wasn't what the goddess of the Underworld was supposed to do, as Father put it. The moment he saw me, he hurried over.

"Whoa, are you okay, Chrys? What happened?"

I shook my head, tears flowing heavier.

Huntley wrapped his arms around me. "Shh, it's okay. You don't need to talk about it. Let's go to your room, alright?"

I nodded, and he helped me to my room. I collapsed on the bean bag chair, still sobbing. I felt pathetic, I *was* pathetic, but I had gotten my hopes up that maybe just this time she would act like she wanted to be with me. That she was happy here. I had been such a fool.

Huntley turned the stereo on and The All-American Rejects started playing. I smiled a bit, as he knew me all too well. He sat down next to me and wrapped his arm around me. I rocked back and forth, trying to let the pain go away.

"She said there was no reason to come to the Underworld. She said she hated it here," I whispered.

Huntley didn't say a word, but I could feel he understood. I wondered if A.J. and Huntley felt the same way, as if they were stuck here and didn't actually want to be here with me, that they had no choice.

"This place isn't that bad, is it? Do you hate it here? Would you leave if you could?" I sniffled.

"No. This place is much better than anything I have ever known. And you alone make it worth it."

I turned to him. Maybe it was the lingering effects of the pomegranate, or the fact I was mad at my parents, but I leaned in, about to kiss him.

Then the door to my room opened.

I had never seen Huntley move so fast. He got up in an instant as my father stepped into my room. He seemed surprised to see Huntley.

"What are you doing here?" he asked him quickly.

Huntley opened his mouth, but nothing came out.

"He saw me crying and was comforting me," I answered for him. "And nothing you can say will make me feel better, Father."

Hades frowned. "Huntley, leave so I can talk to my daughter alone."

I didn't want Huntley to leave, but I knew he wasn't going to disobey my father. He simply nodded and hurried out the door. Hades closed the door and sat down on my bed.

Here we go again.

Chapter 4

Huntley

My parents and I had a lot of fights. I mean, *a lot*. But never had I seen fights like both these gods could get into. I guess when one had an eternity to make up, they just let it all out and waited to see what would happen. However, with the two of them, I knew that they loved each other more than anything else in the end. Hades cared about his daughter more than anything in the universe, and Chrys respected her father more than any other girl I ever knew.

But they were gods, and gods could argue like none other.

I sat outside the door, half wanting to be there for Chrys after her fight with Hades, half wanting to hear the conversation. Fights among the gods were really entertaining and I would put off doing anything just to listen in—that is, if I had something else to do.

I couldn't really make out their words, but could tell Hades was trying to calm his daughter down. He should have probably just left her alone. I knew why he came though: to make sure she wasn't going to let go of her power, destroy everything in this wing of the castle.

Like last time…

She was pretty upset and sometimes when she got upset the unstable emotions she felt took over her powers of self-control. Most of the time she didn't even realize it until her father had successfully woken her out of her trance. I had been there once when it happened. Damn was she powerful.

So that was also another reason I made sure she

was never alone, because I didn't want to see that side of her again. Nor did I think she wanted anyone to see it.

It was scary, to be honest. I didn't know all that she could do, but the shadows she made, the darkness that came out of her. A piece of one of the tendrils had hit my shoulder once when Hades and I were trying to calm her down. It hurt like acid. It was no wonder that A.J. had called it liquid death. It wouldn't have surprised me though, that she could have so much power in her. She was the daughter of Hades, after all.

Another crash. She was going to have to replace that lamp. If this were Earth, she would have been grounded for months. But this wasn't Earth, and Hades had a soft spot for his daughter. That and he knew throwing things was better than her power rising up from deep within and causing even more devastation. Now, if I argued with him, that would be a different story.

The darkness that resided in Chrys was like something out of a fairy tale, like one of the Grimm

Fairy Tales. Although she was nice and kind, she could definitely be the witch and take over all the land if she wanted to. To think that Hades was more powerful scared the shit out of me, though it didn't keep me from getting into trouble. No, that is just why I never got caught.

"Bullshit, Father!" I could actually hear Chrys' voice now. "Stop lying for her! Stop trying to make this better when you know how I feel! When you know that I can't stand her any longer! Why do you even care?"

Another crash. I had to agree with Chrys on this one. Why Hades kept trying to form a bond between his daughter and Persephone was beyond me. It was Persephone that should have come here and talked to her daughter on her own free will. Not Hades.

A couple moments later, Hades stepped out of the room, straightening his tie. I stood up, kind of out of respect, kind of because I was afraid to ever be at a disadvantage. He looked me over, surprised I was still there.

"Were you eavesdropping?" he asked.

I shook my head quickly. "No, just wanted to make sure Chrys was okay after everything."

His eyes narrowed at me, which they always did. "She likes you. Don't know why, but she does. You make her happy."

I didn't know where he was going to go with this, nor even how to respond. *Do I say thanks? Do I say anything?*

Before I could respond, he held out his hand. A bunch of daffodils appeared. "Give these to her, but don't tell her you got them from me. I don't think she wants anything to do with me for a bit."

I took the bunch from his hands. "What's the catch?"

Hades shook his head. "There's no catch. However..." He grabbed my wrist and leaned in closely. "If you make my daughter cry, I will make you suffer for eternity. And that's not an empty threat."

I nodded in haste. "Oh I know, sir. Don't worry."

Letting go of my wrist, he headed down the

hallway, towards Persephone, I presumed. I wondered how that was going to end. They fought a lot, sure, but I had heard things outside their bedroom that have caused me to always go the long way around when she was home. I shuddered at the thought.

I knocked lightly on Chrys' door. She opened it slowly. Her eyes were puffy now, and I slowly raised the flowers with a smile, kind of using them like a shield. "Mind if I come in?"

She looked at the flowers, seeming a bit puzzled by them. "Where did you get those?"

I simply shrugged. "Found them. Thought they might cheer you up."

The one good thing about being a trouble maker was that it caused Chrys never to ask questions. If I were just some nice guy, she would have known that I had gotten them from her father, as he could do weird magic stuff. But since she thought I always stole things, which I did, she figured I stole these too.

Not sure if that really was a good thing, but I told

myself it was.

She opened the door fully and took the flowers. With a snap of her fingers, a black opaque vase with water appeared on her desk and she placed the daffodils on them. She took in a deep breath.

"They have such a sweet smell and are so beautiful." A smile appeared faintly on her lips. Her father was right, that did cheer her up. "Rarely see them when mother is home, however. Everything dies when mother is home."

Well, I tried to get her mind off of it. I rocked on my heels as I peered around her room. Yeah, she had completely destroyed her room. Shards of the broken lamp were all over the floor and there was a big dent marked the wall where she probably nearly hit her father. Some of the pictures she had on her desk were on the floor, the glass broken.

"Gonna take a while to clean all this up, huh?" I asked.

Chrys snapped her fingers and all of it suddenly disappeared and her room looked exactly how it did before the fight. I always forgot she could do that.

"Right. Wish I could have done that growing up. Would have saved me so much time."

Chrys collapsed on the bean bag chair and sighed. I sat next to her and wrapped my arm around her.

"What were your parents like? Did you get along?" she asked.

I laughed. "Hardly. They hated me, thought I was good for nothing. Threw me out of the house just before..." I stopped. I didn't want to tell her how I had died, I couldn't bring myself to admit how stupid I was. I had let so much get under my skin when I should have just ran for my life. "Anyway, I know how you feel about your parents. It's only natural. As for your dad, he's really a nice guy. He cares about you more than anything."

"Yeah, I know." She leaned her head on my shoulder. "We get along all the time, except when *she's* home. Then we always fight about her."

"Just know that he would never kick you out."

She laughed. "He doesn't really have anywhere to kick me to."

"True, but either way he wouldn't. That's

something to always think on." I sucked at this consoling thing, but knew I couldn't just leave her feeling so sad. "Besides, most people fight when they are around each other for long periods of time."

"We don't fight," she commented. "At least, I don't remember us ever having a fight. Why's that?"

She got me there. There wasn't a person on Earth that I met that I didn't get in a fight with. Chrys was the only exception, but then again she wasn't on Earth.

Could I feel more for her than I realized?

"Uh, not sure. Guess we just have personalities that go well together."

She bit her lip as she looked at me. She was full of emotions, confused, everything swirling in her mind. That had to be the reason she looked as if she wanted to kiss me, but wasn't sure she wanted to. I debated moving away, not letting her make a mistake out of anger, but at the same time I wanted to kiss her so badly. She leaned in a little closer.

"Heard the yelling, what's going on?" A.J.

appeared in the doorway at the worst time. Chrys stood up and wiped away some of the tears that were still on her face.

Fuck, I couldn't get a break.

"Why are you here?" I glared at him.

A.J. stepped to Chrys, wiping away the last tear. "I heard things break and yelling, wanted to make sure Chrys was okay. Figured she got in a fight with Hades about Persephone again."

"I'm fine," she sighed. "Just the normal fight we always have. I just can't stand that woman. I hate it when she's here."

"You know Persephone has been cursed to come here. It's not your fault she hates it. She's the daughter of the goddess of harvest and fertility. I don't know if you have noticed, but this place is the complete opposite," A.J. commented. He gave her a little smile. "But she doesn't see how special you are. She doesn't see what the rest of us do. That this place is worth it to be with you."

I rolled my eyes. That's what I was going to say, but at least I really meant it. This guy, I don't know.

Something made me feel like he was planning something. That he was using her. But what that was, I had no idea. It wasn't like he made any advances on her or anything, especially since it had been thousands of years that they knew one another, so it wasn't her specifically that he was after. But what it was, I had no idea...

"You don't have a choice. You and Huntley are stuck here," Chrys sighed.

"Well, either way. I wouldn't try to leave this place if given the opportunity."

Chrys smiled at his comment. I about gagged. I hated it when he acted all sweet to her. He was just like all those dicks I knew in my mortal life, using people for their own devices. But they had known each other for four thousand years, what did I know?

Oh right, I knew a douche when I saw one.

I stood up. "I wish you were able to vacation away from this place, visit Earth. But honestly, it isn't that great. Bunch of idiots and selfish people."

"Yeah, well," Chrys said. "Not much different

down here." She bit her lip, as if thinking. "If I did want to leave, if I wanted to get away for a couple of days, would you two go with me?" she whispered.

I stared at her. *Was she really thinking about sneaking off to Earth?* I couldn't believe it if that were the case. Before I came, she never got into trouble. She never disobeyed her father. Yes, they fought just like they had been fighting, but her imagining running away, that wasn't like her at all.

Or maybe she was just more open about it. That happened, you know, when emotions and thoughts were suppressed for so long and they were finally able to be set free.

"I don't know, Chrys, if you got caught by Zeus, wouldn't you be destroyed? Isn't that why your father doesn't want you to leave?" I asked. *Surprised?* Yeah, I was a bit too. But it wasn't like this was just getting into a bit of trouble. If something went wrong, it would mean she would be done for. She would experience eternal torment in Tartarus, or at least that's what I gathered from all that Hades hinted about. And Hades wouldn't be able to do anything about it, as Zeus was the god of gods. He could do whatever he wanted.

"I would follow you," A.J. answered. "I know you wouldn't go about it carelessly. Just for a couple of days, I doubt we would even get caught."

I couldn't believe what I was hearing. I turned to him. "Are you nuts? She can't leave this place. And what do you mean not get caught? Can't Zeus see everything on Earth? He would see that she's a goddess, look at her."

"A goddess can mask what she is. I doubt he would notice; the world is a big place. Besides, Hades is a pessimist. I really doubt anything bad would happen."

I looked back at Chrys. "But you aren't serious, right? I mean, I would do whatever I could to help but even I can see it's a bad idea, and that's saying a lot."

She bit her lip. "Yeah, you're right. It's not a good idea. I'm just pissed, that's all. I wouldn't do something so reckless. But I'm tired. If you two wouldn't mind, I would like to retire for the night."

We both nodded and went to leave her room.

"Good night, Chrys," I said.

She smiled as she shut the door slowly behind us. "Look forward to tutoring tomorrow. Goodnight."

The door closed, leaving just A.J. and me standing there awkwardly. I turned to A.J. "What the hell was that?"

"What are you talking about?" he asked as he started to turn to leave.

I grabbed him and pushed him against the wall. "What do you mean? You know *exactly* what I am talking about."

A.J. glanced at where my hand was touching. "Please remove your hand before I permanently remove it."

I let go of him. If he were human, I would have accepted his challenge. But he was a demigod. He had a bit of an advantage.

"Seriously, dude, what are you thinking?" I whispered.

He let out a breath, as if dealing with me was a chore. "Look, I've known about gods longer than you can even comprehend. If we were on Earth for just a couple of days, there is no chance that anyone would find out. Hades just worries a lot because he's overprotective of her, which I can understand knowing Zeus and my father."

"Oh," I whispered. It was hard to keep track, I admitted, of all the gods and goddesses and how this world of the immortals worked. But he had a lot of time to learn these things, many mortal lifetimes. I tried to understand it but there was a lot of complexity contained in the idea of multiple lifetimes.

"So, if she wants to leave, let her. Between the two of us she would be safe, right?"

I nodded slowly. I still felt uneasy about everything, but he knew more about this world than I did. If he said it was safe, then maybe it was.

"Well, there you have it. Now stop arguing with me." He turned and left.

I watched as he left. He never complimented me like that, ever. There *had* to be something else going on.

Chapter 5

Chrys

I got over being mad at Father. *Eventually*.

A couple of weeks passed since the fight happened. I had been trying my best to ignore Mother, not even be seen by her. If she came to my room, I tried my best to hide, to disappear, or make the excuse that I was busy studying with Huntley. It had worked, as she hadn't reached out for a couple of days.

Father and I had been spending more time together, alone. He never brought up the fight, and I didn't particularly want to remind him. He seemed understanding, as the fate of the gods were a complicated one. We could hold grudges like none other, though, seeing as how we had an eternity to sort it all out.

I didn't have to help judge and sit at the throne with Hades, as mother was home now. She was the Queen of the Underworld, at least for three months of the year. She was to help judge now and when she left, I could once again help my father and learn how his reign works. Yes, I had been here for a long while, but he really didn't seem to care until recently. I didn't know why that was; I figured he probably just wanted to take a vacation or something.

Instead, the two of us spent some time after his work, playing games, conversing over tea, and watching movies. I loved being able to hang out like this, like what I imagined humans did for their leisure. Huntley had said that he didn't know any human that had a bond like Hades and I did, but liked to think that's what it was like out there. I hadn't known many families, at least ones that were alive. I had only heard stories of the gods, of how they defeated the Titans. I guess I was lucky to have such a great dad compared to my father's. And my mother was alright I guess, as long as I didn't have to see her or deal with her melodramatic crap.

Today we were playing poker, Texas Holdem to be exact. A.J. and Huntley had joined us, as two-player Texas Holdem wasn't nearly as fun. We sat at a small table, each with green visors and popcorn, like in the movies. Huntley seemed reluctant about the visors, but in the end he didn't care.

Hades shuffled the cards in one hand, as he had a lot of time to practice, while Huntley tapped his fingers on the table.

"So what's the chips get us in the end? Is this for actual money or chores or something?" Huntley asked. He seemed to be enjoying himself, since he couldn't sit still.

My father stared at him as he kept shuffling. "They aren't for anything. We already don't do chores and money is worthless down here."

"Well that's no fun. You know on Earth sometimes they play betting with their clo—"

I kicked him in the shin before he could finish that innuendo. I didn't know what my father would say to that, or do to Huntley for even suggesting it.

"Well, this isn't Earth," A.J. commented. He always seemed fast to remind Huntley of that.

"It was just a suggestion," Huntley replied. "I'm just trying to lighten the mood."

"No you are just opening your mouth when it should remain shut," A.J. snapped back.

I clapped my hands together. I was trying to get away from arguing and people wanted to wring each other's necks. They weren't really as bad as Mother and Father though, mainly Mother. "Okay, how about you deal so we can start this game, Father."

He gave Huntley a mutinous look, then proceeded with a wave of his hand to pass out the first two cards. I received an eight of diamonds and a ten of spades. Unless a nine or something like that was going to show up, this was complete crap.

"Flower, you start."

I knocked on the table to pass. There was no way I was going to bid on this, unless I just wanted to bluff. Not a good idea this early in the game. I learned that over the years of playing against my Father.

Mother never liked to play games, at least not with us. She probably played all sorts of games with her men. Great Cronus, I didn't want to think about that. I needed to get my head back in the game.

Everyone else passed, and Father turned over the flop. It was a four of spades, two of hearts, and a four of clubs. Even more crap for my hand. I should fold, but I didn't want to give up this early in the game.

I glanced over at Huntley as I munched on some popcorn. He appeared as bummed as I did. A.J., on the other hand, looked intense. He probably had something. He was so easy to read.

Betting a white chip, the lowest price, I watched as Huntley reluctantly placed one as well, A.J. appearing to be thinking about raising it but decided not to, and Hades matched. Father turned over another card. Four of diamonds.

I checked because, let's be honest, I had nothing good in my hand. Huntley did the same.

"I bet five." A.J. placed a red chip on the table.

"Fold," I said. Both Huntley and Hades did the same.

A.J. took the four white chips and his red chip. "Sweet, first round is mine."

Huntley said, either irritated that he lost or that A.J. had won. "What kind of dealing was that, Hades? Do you know how to shuffle?"

Huntley never knew when to shut up, but at least we were all having fun so anything he said Father wouldn't hold against him, at least not for that long. Father glared at him and a chip from his pile went flying and hit Huntley in the middle of his forehead.

"What the—" Huntley rubbed his forehead. "That was uncalled for. Also, I'm keeping that chip."

"Just shut up, will you?" A.J. turned to me. "Your turn to deal, Chrys."

I bit my lip as I grabbed the cards. I had the power

to make it so I could win, but that wasn't fun. I liked winning because of luck and skill. I shuffled the cards with one hand, just as Father had done, raising my eyebrow at Huntley.

"Yeah, yeah. Showoff."

I laughed as I dealt the first two cards. A five of hearts and nine of hearts. Not bad, at least they were of the same suit. I hoped that the flop would be better than last time. It was really nice to have a day like this where I could just relax and not think about my mother. I wished she would go back to Earth so we could relax and enjoy ourselves. But no, three more months. Three. More. Months.

"Huntley, do you bet anything?" I asked.

He shook his head. "No, I check."

A.J. and Hades did the same, and I turned over the flop. A two of diamonds, six of diamonds, and a King of spades. Nothing good. Maybe I should have used my powers this turn, in the most discreet way possible.

"White chip," Huntley said as he tossed a chip in the pile.

I grabbed a handful of popcorn and began to munch on it. I loved popcorn, it was so fluffy. Kernels sucked though, I always got them stuck in my teeth.

"I'm going to meet that and raise you to a red." A.J. tossed in a red. Hades and I both met the bid amount. Huntley just stared at A.J.

"Actually have something or did you just want to up me?"

A.J. shrugged as Huntley traded his white chip for a red one. I flipped over the next card, and it was an Ace of diamonds.

Huntley seemed to perk up. Figured he must have a diamond, only needing one more to get a flush. Anyone could have a flush at this point.

"Hmm, wonder if anyone has a flush," I commented as I bit my lip.

Huntley placed down a red chip, smiling. "You better fold, if you aren't sure."

"Who says I don't have a flush? Maybe I have the King as well, then you would be screwed," I teased. He seemed to hesitate for a moment, but simply smiled.

"You don't, you're such a bad liar."

A.J. interrupted our jest. "I'll call your bet."

Father also placed down a red chip. "So do I, and I have to agree with Huntley, you are a terrible liar."

Huntley smiled. "So we do agree on something? Good to know." I sided with Huntley. It was really rare for them to agree on something, but it, of course, had to be at my expense.

I flipped over another card. It was the Jack of diamonds. So pretty much if anyone has a diamond, I was screwed.

"First blue chip of the night," Huntley flipped in a chip, a smile apparent on his face. Gee, I wonder what card he had.

A.J. threw in his cards. "I fold. Hades?"

Hades stared at Huntley for a moment, debating. "I'll meet it."

I threw in my own cards. "Well, I fold. Guess you all are right, I suck at lying."

Huntley bit his lip as he slowly laid out his cards. "Four of diamonds, eight of hearts. A flush."

Hades turned over his card as well. It was Queen of clubs and a nine of diamonds. "I have a flush as well."

"But… then who wins?" Huntley asked.

"Hades does, you moron," A.J. said. "His nine trumps your four."

Huntley threw his cards in the pile and leaned back in his chair. "Fuck!"

I saw a hint of a smile appear on Father's lips. He never smiled when Huntley was around, I was glad he was finally starting to warm up to him, even though it was because Hades crushed his hopes with this game.

It was also nice to see Father enjoying himself. He rarely seemed to have fun, especially when Mother was home. He deserved happiness, especially after everything his brothers have put him through.

"Should have thought about it more carefully, Huntley. Four is a low card. You were at a disadvantage with that flop if someone else had a diamond," Hades explained as he took in his pile.

"Whatever," Huntley muttered. "My turn to deal

right?"

I nodded. "Yup. Now make this one count."

Huntley mumbled something under his breath, but I didn't quite hear it. Probably a few more curse words.

"Sorry I have to shuffle the mortal way with two hands, and not use magic to pass them out," Huntley said as he shuffled with both his hands and the table. I laughed a little as he started to pass them out.

I had a six of clubs and a Jack of spades. Not the greatest hand, but it could work out to my advantage for me in the end. Huntley could barely stay still with whatever he had. Probably a pair or something.

"A.J., you start," I said as I grabbed some more popcorn.

"I'm going to check. Hades?"

"Same," Father said.

I nodded, and Huntley tossed over the flop. It was a two of diamonds, six of spades, and four of hearts. It was A.J. this time who seemed to get excited and more into the game, as I did with the six of spades. Hades, well, he always kept his cool while playing a game. Unless he got angry, then he usually destroyed whatever we were playing, which is why we no longer play Aggravation.

"I bet a blue," A.J. said. Each of us met it. Apparently we all had something of worth, which I knew required me to exercise caution.

Huntley turned over the next card. A six of hearts. Now I had three of a kind.

"Green chip this time," A.J. placed in a green chip. I bit my lip as Father did the same.

"Someone has something really good. Don't know what to do," I said, acting as if I didn't have something, or did. I just liked talking and throwing people off.

"We all know you have nothing, just give me your chips and we will call it good," Huntley teased.

"I don't know, maybe this time around I have something good. You really never know. It would be something you would do, giving me a really good hand without realizing it. I call." I tossed in a green chip, and Huntley did the same.

"Your funeral," he commented as he turned over the next card. It was a ten of hearts. So far I still had a three of a kind.

A.J. tossed in a red. So he probably didn't get what he had hoped for. I most likely had him beat this time. Father also tossed in a red. I really didn't know if he had anything.

"I'll meet that. Come on Huntley, toss in your red so I can take it all," I commented.

He laughed. "As if." Huntley tossed in the red chip.

"Two pair, fours and sixes," A.J. said.

"Same." Hades turned his cards over.

I grinned widely. "Three sixes. Ha!" I turned to Huntley. "And you?"

He was frowning. "Two pair, eights and sixes. Damn it!" He threw his cards in.

I laughed as I took in all the chips. "You suck at this Huntley. You barely have any chips left."

"Yeah, yeah. A.J.'s turn to deal."

A.J. gathered the cards and started shuffling them

like Huntley.

"See, sucks to be mortal, huh?" Huntley commented.

A.J. gave him a look. "I'm a demigod, not a mortal. Get it right."

Huntley shrugged. "Either way, you have to shuffle those like a mortal."

A.J. passed out the cards. I had an Ace of diamonds and a seven of diamonds. Two diamonds, that would come in handy.

"Hades, do you bet anything?" A.J. asked.

He shook his head. "No."

"I do, one white." I tossed it on the table.

"Gonna be like that, eh?" Huntley tossed in a chip. "Only jerks bet pre-flop."

"Well maybe I'm a jerk."

I could tell Huntley was holding back a snarky comment, probably because my father was there. A.J. and Hades met the bet, and the flop was turned over. Six of clubs, seven of spades, and an eight of clubs.

Maybe I shouldn't have bet pre-flop. I was hoping

for a flush, but at least I had two sevens. Father put down a white chip. He didn't have anything.

"Raise to a blue chip," I smiled at Father.

"Raising the stakes. I can get behind that." Huntley added his chip and so did A.J.

Hades stared at me for a moment, then put down his hand. "I fold."

I took a bite of some more popcorn, happy that I had defeated my father and made him fold. The next card down was a King of hearts, which was worthless. I put down a red, and everyone matched. Next card was a six of diamonds. Now I had two pair.

"Blue chip." I glanced at Huntley. He shook his head.

"Fold. I only get crap hands, I swear."

"I'll meet your bid, Chrys." A.J. didn't seem to waver. He had something. Again.

I flipped over my cards. "Two pair."

A.J. flipped his cards over. "So do I, eight high."

"Damn it!" I threw in my cards and went to grab another handful of popcorn. The bowl was empty.

Standing up, I grabbed the bowl. "I'm going to get some more popcorn."

Hades started to get up. "I can do that—"

"No," I said. "You shuffle and deal. I will be right back. Give me some good cards this time. Anyone want some more beer?"

Everyone but A.J. wanted another, and I hurried off towards the kitchen as I heard the cards begin to be shuffled for another round. The anxiety of my forthcoming turn spiked my adrenaline. I loved popcorn and was most definitely going to get a stomach ache between that and the beer, both great distractions away from the tension brought on by my mother.

I sat on the counter as I waited for the popcorn to finish. As it stopped popping for a few seconds, I opened the microwave and pulled out the bag. Luckily I didn't get burnt from hot things, which always threw Huntley off when he grabbed something after me. He healed quickly. It was the Underworld after all, but not after a few curse words brought on by the pain.

Opening the fridge, I grabbed four beer bottles. The bottle opener was in the game room, so I didn't have to worry about opening them, and most likely spilling them everywhere.

My hands full, I hurried back to the game room. As I passed by one of the spare rooms, I could hear my mom giggling. Suddenly the door opened in front of me and she stepped out in a robe... With another man.

Chapter 6

Huntley

"You slut!" I heard Chrys scream from the hallway. I glanced up at Hades whose body I could tell instantly tensed at those jarring words. He had worked so hard to get her to smile again, to get her to calm down. He even let A.J. and I play games with the two of them to lift her spirits. Now it was all in vain.

"I knew I should have had one of you two get the popcorn," he mumbled. He appeared to be indecisive about whether he should get up and tend to her or not, sort of starting to stand up but not really. So I made the decision for him.

I got up and headed towards the hallway. It was probably better that I went after her compared to Hades as he and Persephone would just start fighting again. She only did this to piss him off, but unfortunately it only hurt their daughter in the long run.

I found Chrys throwing beer bottles at the guy who was just in his boxers. There was popcorn everywhere. Okay, I knew it wasn't my business, but Persephone could definitely be a little more discrete about it all. Did she ever think it through, though? Also, this place was huge, couldn't she just use one of the bedrooms on the other side of the palace?

"Chrys, please stop!" Persephone yelled, but kept out of the way of Chrys' oncoming wrath. Chrys was definitely the goddess of the Underworld. You didn't want to piss her off, or there would be hell to pay. *Literally.*

"You fucking whore!" she yelled, tears falling

from her face, her eyeliner creating streaks down her face, making her look even more terrifying, honestly. Though she could be scary, and hurt anything around her, I knew I would never turn my back on her. I couldn't. I owed her that much. My life, or life after death, was in her hands and she could honestly do as she pleased. It would be better than what I suffered on Earth.

Wind started whipping around her dark hair, growing more and more strong. It felt like a tornado beginning to form, a tornado of power as the crackle of static electricity sounded. Dark shadows began to appear in the air, the light from the chandeliers in the hallways was almost completely extinguished.

Ah, crap. Not again.

So if I had a daughter who would control life and death, I probably wouldn't piss her off to the extent where she might kill whoever I had snuck into the Underworld. Even I could figure that out. I hated how she was caught in the middle of whatever was going on between Hades and Persephone. She was probably just pissing off her daughter to get under

Hades skin. That or she was completely stupid.

Darkness was completely pouring out of Chrys now. Her eyes were black, almost as if possessed by a demon like on all those supernatural shows. It was her own darkness, though, the darkness that always resided within her. She couldn't control it, she wasn't the master of it, and sometimes she let it out of its cage. Like right now, for instance. We were all doomed unless I did something quickly.

And, you know, didn't die again in the process.

Black tendrils swung out around her and Persephone and the idiot man who easily fell for her good looks got out of the way. I, however, wasn't so lucky.

Fuck that hurts.

I bit back the pain as the spot on my shoulder where it hit turned black with death. It would heal, eventually. My shoulder would just be sore for a few days. However, if I didn't act now, I would be in a lot more pain.

As fast as I could, I grabbed Chrys's waist and threw her over my shoulder. The wind stopped, but she was definitely still angry. She punched and kicked, but at least she wasn't going to make the hallway explode anymore. A few kicks and punches were definitely better than *that*.

I brought her into the room we were playing poker in and slammed the door shut with my foot, but not before Hades saw the guy Persephone was with. I couldn't tell if he was pissed about Persephone sleeping with another guy or that she let herself be caught by their daughter. I don't think I could deal with that kind of shit if I were him, especially if I were the god of the Underworld. He was fucking *Hades*, for crying out loud.

I let Chrys down as she had calmed herself down a lot, taking deep breaths. A.J. and Hades stayed at the table, waiting to see if she was alright. Hades didn't want to interfere again, in fear that they would get in a fight. He did, however, see my shoulder but didn't say a word. He knew I was in excruciating pain and that his daughter hadn't noticed what she had done yet. With a snap of his fingers, a jacket appeared on me. I nodded a thank you, grimacing a bit as it was rubbing on the wound.

Rubbing Chrys' arms, I said. "Chrys, breath. Everything is okay now."

Tears stopped falling from her eyes, and she nodded. "I'm okay. Thanks. Sorry, I almost lost it."

I shrugged. "It's fine. No worries."

She turned to the table with a deep breath. "Finish our games then? I seemed to have dropped the beer and popcorn."

A.J. stood up. "I will go get some more. You can sit down."

Chrys nodded as she took a seat. I could hear the crunch of glass under A.J.'s shoe as he walked through the broken beer bottles. I sat back down across from Hades as Chrys stared at her cards, lost in the thought of everything.

Hades mouthed "thank you". I simply nodded. It wasn't like I could let Chrys fight her demons alone. I owed that much to her, I knew.

Believe it or not, I lost all my chips by the end of the

game. Yeah, if this was golf or something, I would have been really well off.

Chrys had the most chips, which I had a feeling was her father's doing, as every hand he dealt she won. How he could do that, I wasn't really sure. But he was a god, so it wasn't all that surprising that he manipulated things to let Chrys win in the end. He would do anything to make her smile.

She didn't talk much during the rest of the night of playing games. She seemed to be lost in her own world, thinking about everything that just happened. I supposed after thousands of years of dealing with that kind of crap, I would be pretty pissed too.

Hades let A.J. and I walk her back to her room after the game. I wished I had some pomegranate seeds to give her, but they were hard to come by when Persephone was home. I had a feeling she had them a lot.

My arm still hurt, by the way. The wound was hidden beneath the jacket I wore and I tried not to think about it, but god it hurt. Bad. And it was going to take a while to heal.

I could hear Hades and Persephone arguing from down the hallway. There were some things being thrown, I could tell, but had no idea by whom. Probably Persephone as Hades didn't seem like someone who would ever throw something at his wife or daughter. Other people, yes. He made that clear when he threw the poker chip at my face.

Chrys pretended not to hear them, but it was clear she could. Her body was still tense, and she was quiet. I glanced at A.J., wondering if he knew what to do. He simply shrugged.

We made it to Chrys' room, and she plopped on her bed. I didn't know if she wanted us to leave right away or if she wanted to talk. We both kind of just stood there, waiting for any kind of signal.

"We should run away," she whispered. "For just a little bit, like A.J. said."

I was hoping she had gotten the idea of running away out of her head by now. It didn't feel like a good idea to me. It scared me that the god of the Underworld was afraid of Zeus. It could only mean bad things would happen if we went to Earth.

And the fact Earth just sucked was another reason. Mortals were selfish bastards who didn't care about anyone but themselves. I would know: I was one of them.

"Chrys, I don't think-" I began, but A.J. cut me off.

"If you think it would help, we can both go with you, *right* Huntley?"

I glared at him. I didn't care how much more he knew about the world of the gods than me, I really doubted this was a good idea. Persephone would be gone in a couple of months, and Chrys would be fine then. But I knew that curiosity would have gotten the better of me as well, if I were in her situation, never having been anywhere but the underworld for so many years. "I will go with you, yes. But do you really think it's a good idea? I mean your father would freak out if he noticed you were missing."

Chrys sat up in her bed. "Not if he thought I was somewhere else."

"What do you mean?" I asked. Because I didn't

think she could go anywhere else. I thought she was trapped in the Underworld.

She nodded her head, as if actually planning something out. *Shit.*

"If I left a note saying that we had gone over to one of the other gods of the Underworld's place, he would probably leave us alone. He wouldn't know we were on Earth. Though he doesn't particularly like me even anywhere outside of the palace, I don't think he would mind given the current state of things."

"There are other gods here?" I asked. I really had no idea. No one took much time to try to explain things to me, as they seriously assumed I took Greek Mythology in high school. Newsflash, they rarely offered that in any school.

"Like Maka. You haven't visited her lately," A.J. commented. "And the Furies."

Chrys nodded her head. "Yeah, we used to hang out there all the time until she got really busy."

"Who's Maka?" I asked.

"Makaria. She's kind of like a sister. Hades

created her out of the need for a governess of the blessed souls, those who did good in the human world. Some gods think she's Hades' daughter, but she's more like a creation than anything."

I tried to straighten that out since no one bothered telling me earlier. "But if she's like a daughter of Hades, to the other gods anyway, why would anyone have a problem with him actually having a daughter. Why does he try to hide you but not her?"

A.J. answered that one. "Because the power that Chrys has is a lot more than any other god in Olympus. Maka can't do too much. With Chrys' father actually being Hades and her mother being Persephone, she has the ability to control life and death. Zeus has already destroyed one person who brought people back to life. It wasn't natural, so Zeus wouldn't allow it. He is really strict about his laws, as he is the god of order and nature."

I let out a sigh. It still didn't make sense, but I decided to go with it. "Okay, so I take it then that this Maka doesn't have nearly as much power as you."

"No," Chrys said as she opened up her desk drawer. "Like I said, she's kind of like a governess." She took everything out of her drawer and pulled back the bottom, revealing a hidden part of the drawer. Three silver rings with garnet gems sat at the bottom.

A.J.'s eyes widened. "No way. How did you manage to get a hold of those?"

"What are those?" I asked. Because honestly, they just looked like normal rings.

Chrys picked them up. "They're rings to get us through the River Styx. Father made them for Persephone so she could cross over when she went to Earth. However, she tends to lose them, as in she gives them to men so they can visit her. It wasn't hard getting a hold of a few over the years."

"So if you just left a note, at this point your father would just assume you were there, he would leave you alone. We could leave and come back without anyone noticing." I could see A.J.'s eyes sparkle now. He wanted this a little too much.

I still didn't think it was a good idea, I mean

going behind Hades' back wasn't a good idea no matter how foolproof the plan was. I didn't particularly want to piss him off, especially since I was finally on his good side after everything. It had taken a very long time to do that. Well, kind of. A long time for me, as in a few years in mortal time, would seem like nothing to them.

Chrys nodded her head quickly. "Yes. Let's do it. Before dawn, we should leave. I know how to get a boat, that will be the least of our problems."

I stepped up to Chrys, placing my hand on her shoulder and looked her straight in the eyes. "This isn't a good idea. The Earth sucks, Chrys, nothing good can come of this. Are you sure you want to risk everything?"

For a moment I thought I had squeezed some sense into her. She appeared to actually be thinking about it when A.J. slapped my shoulder, right where the wound was. *Fuuuuuuuucccccckkkkkk.* He was going to get an earful from me later, I swore.

A.J. said, "It will be fine. She has the two of us. She deserves to see what the world is like. It may have been cruel to you, Huntley, but to a god it can be so much more."

Chrys glanced over at A.J. and smiled. "Yeah, he's right. It has to be perfect if my mother would choose it over me."

I wondered if that was the real reason she wanted to go to the Earth, to see what her mother would rather have than being with both her daughter and husband Hades. Hades seemed like a really good guy, for being the god of the Underworld and all. I couldn't imagine any human being better than him though, I surely hadn't ever met a guy who would go to such lengths to keep their girl happy. I wondered if it had to do something with him once having an affair with another woman. I wish I knew more details about that, but I didn't dare ask.

I sighed. "Fine. Just tell me when and where to meet."

Chapter 7

Chrys

The River Styx is really intimidating. Like, *seriously*.

I honestly had never realized it until now, being without someone who knew how to guide the boat for me. I had only taken a boat out a couple of times, but never this far, and never with this much risk. Now that I stood here, waiting for the others, I found myself questioning my decision a little bit. Not enough to turn back, but enough to realize that Father was going to be really pissed if he found out I had hijacked a boat and left the Underworld with two of my friends. I guess I knew that already, but it was hitting me hard now.

I had left a note for him, telling him we were going to visit Maka and not to worry, that we would be back in a few days. He knew I needed to let off a little steam and that leaving me alone was the best choice. At least, I hoped.

I was already wearing my ring and waiting to give A.J. and Huntley theirs. I was almost past the point of no return, making a decision that could get me in the worst of trouble.

And it felt exhilarating.

I was surprised that Huntley wasn't fully on board with this, but more cautious than A.J. and I were. He was only coming because he wanted to make sure I was safe. But if A.J. thought it would be fine, I really doubted it was going to end badly.

At least I hoped that it wouldn't.

A.J. was the cautious one out of the three of us, so if Huntley thought it was fine, it was probably going to be fine. I trusted him, especially after all this time. He cared enough to stay in the Palace for me, so he had to be speaking the truth.

A.J. and Huntley showed up, checking behind them to make sure there wasn't anyone following them. I nodded to both of them and handed them the rings. They slipped them on their fingers, and we quickly climbed in the boat to travel around the River Styx into the sky that was Oceanus.

The boat was like an old gondola that might simply crumble if we were going over actual water. It was beyond old, probably the same age as the Underworld itself. It creaked and cracked as we stood on it, rocking slightly back and forth. The three of us each grabbed a stick and pushed off the pier of the palace and into the river we went.

"How does this actually work?" Huntley asked. "I mean, it looks like we are traveling on clouds."

"Are you really going to ask questions of how things work in the Underworld? Not just accept that things work differently here?" A.J. replied. We had barely been gone for a couple of moments and they were already arguing.

"The rivers here are more like air currents,

trapping things that have been lost in the mortal realm," I explained. "The river we are on now is the River Styx, the River of Hatred. It is but one of five rivers. Most of the dead come to this world via Acheron, the River of Pain. It is where Charon runs his service. The other rivers flow through the Underworld and serve as transportation to places throughout. But without a boat, all the rivers will curse those who try to escape, so make sure the water doesn't touch you."

Huntley glanced over the water, his eyes wide. I probably should have mentioned that earlier, but it had completely slipped my mind. When you knew something for such a long time, it was hard to remember to tell others who might not know.

"Don't worry, you're fine. But because of this, no god from the other realms can get through Oceanus, which is why Father has hidden me away for so long. That is, except Hermes, he can travel between realms. Why that is, no one really knows. He kinda just appears some days and Father can't figure out how he's doing it. As for my mother, well, it's really rare for anyone to come to the Underworld and be able to go back to Earth. In some legends the hero can, or antagonist, depending on your point of view. The River Styx was their greatest obstacle."

"But she sneaks men in here," Huntley countered.

I nodded. "Yeah, but they don't come by themselves. She pays Charon to escort them. He will escort anything as long as he gets paid."

"Oh. So which one is the River Styx?" Huntley asked.

I gestured in front of us. "This one. We will be going around the Underworld seven times and then be dumped into Oceanus."

"Seven times? Won't that take forever?"

I shrugged. "Space is weird here. Doesn't take too long actually and the farther we get, the faster it starts to go."

"Oh, I guess that makes sense," Huntley said. "Then where is Oceanus?"

I nodded up. "You see, the blue clouds that covers the entire realm? That's Oceanus."

He looked up at the sky. The molten blue

shimmered in the light of the morning. Where the morning light really came from, I still wasn't sure. This world was weird, I had to agree.

"Shit. How are we supposed to get through that?" he asked.

"Hence the boat, moron," A.J. commented.

Huntley pointed up. "Yeah, but that doesn't have a surface that we can travel on."

I shook my head. "That's because we don't travel on it. We travel through it. Oceanus is like a shell between this world and Earth."

"Oh yeah, that's going to be fun. Do you even know where we are going to end up?"

I was silent. I actually didn't. I figured, probably wherever my mother was last, but I couldn't be sure. It wasn't like I had a preference. Anywhere was better than here. Finally, I shrugged.

"We don't even know where we are going?" Huntley exclaimed. "Chrys, seriously, get some sense in your head. This is a *bad* idea."

He was right, I really didn't know what I was doing. I should turn back now, I had let my emotions get the better of me. I was turning into my mother.

And I didn't want that.

This whole trip was to prove to myself that I wasn't like my mother, that I didn't care about the other worlds, but it was quite the opposite. I was acting like her, sneaking out and potentially making Father worry. I couldn't believe what I was doing. Was I really turning out to be like her? No, that was impossible. I loathed her ways with every fiber of my being.

So then why was I risking everything for this trip away from the Underworld?

Before I could say anything, A.J. intervened. "It will be fine. If you didn't want to come, then you should have stayed home. We aren't going to be gone long and we have these rings to get back. I've seen her mother and Hermes do it a million times, not to mention all the men that Persephone sneaks in. If those humans and demigods can get through that river, so can we."

I shot him a look for bringing up all my mother's

affairs. I really didn't want to think about that right now.

He simply shrugged. "Hey, it's true. If they can do this, then so can we."

I sighed. He definitely had a point. None of those men were particularly powerful. If they could make it through with those rings, then so could we. Even if we didn't have Charon at our side.

As we traveled down the River Styx, something appeared in the cloud in front of us. A body floating in the water, heading towards the palace. It was a young girl, probably no older than fifteen, her eyes open, full of fright. She was trying to say something, screaming for help, but no sound was coming out. I wanted to look away, not to empathize with her pain, but I couldn't move my eyes from her.

The person was to be judged, I knew, and not having Charon guiding them, it could take centuries for the body to drift where it needed to go. It sickened me, honestly, and if it were up to me, I would send search parties out every day to gather them. In fact, I had even gone out and saved a few from being lost for centuries.

"What's that?" Huntley asked.

"A lost soul. Someone who died under circumstances of his or her feeling lost. Souls like that usually drift for a long while until Charon comes across them or one of the Erinyes. Then they are judged depending on their circumstances," I explained, not really wanting to go on any further. I should have thought before I spoke, but now it was too late.

"What do you mean a lost soul?" he asked.

I bit my lip, debating if I should say, but I knew I couldn't lie. "One that potentially killed themselves to be here, whether it be on purpose or by accident."

He stopped talking. I knew something like that had to have happened to him, as this was where I spotted him one day from my bedroom window. I quickly grabbed A.J. and he helped me pull him out of the river, though A.J. did protest the entire time. I snuck him into the palace and told Father that Huntley simply appeared to be my next mentor, as I had many over the years to learn about human culture. He didn't appear to actually believe me, but I could always win my father over with a convincing enough smile.

I never told Huntley that was where I found him, and he still might not know. But after explaining why our boat just went past a soul that had been floating in the water, he probably put two and two together. I felt bad for those souls, as I knew most of them were destined for the Field of Asphodel, but they had to be found first. Though not all of them went there. And that was why I took Huntley under my protection from my Father, before he could be judged to go somewhere far worse.

But now that he was with us, served time as my mentor, he could go to the Elysian Fields. That was where all the souls of my tutors went, as a reward if they weren't already destined there. I hadn't told Huntley this yet, as he would probably choose paradise over staying with me in the palace. It was selfish, yes, but he had brought me so much happiness that I couldn't let him go. I couldn't go back to being so lonely again.

We came closer and closer to Oceanus. Goosebumps appeared on my arms and I felt a chill in the air. If my father spotted us, I would have already known. With a snap of his finger, we would have appeared back in the palace, his wrath consuming us. We would face a stiff penalty. But it was quiet. He really had no idea that we had snuck out right under his nose.

He was probably too busy arguing with Persephone some more. I had heard them last night, all night actually, Persephone throwing things at him as if it were all his fault that she could never find lasting happiness. Then again, I did the same thing when he tried to talk to me too. It seems I adopted some characteristic of my mother then.

I didn't like comparing myself to her, as I noticed more similarities between the two of us than I cared to admit. I wanted to be different from her, I wanted to show that I wouldn't follow in her footsteps.

Maybe going to Earth wasn't the best thing to do. It was what she would have done in my place; it is kind of what she always did.

I wasn't acting like her, I wasn't trying to escape this place. I was trying to escape *her*. It had nothing to do with not loving this world, with not getting along with my father. It had to do with her saying that Earth was better than being with me. I wanted to know first-hand whether this was true.

I kept that in my mind as we approached Oceanus. It looked like a starry sky, at least from what I had seen from pictures. It looked so beautiful.

But I knew it was going to hurt like hell. Because, let's be honest, didn't everything in the Underworld hurt like hell?

"Hold on!" I screamed as the gondola started to pierce through the veil. The gondola shook, thrashing us about. The water, or whatever this shell was made out of, engulfed us. I could hardly breathe as I was thrown down to the bench of the boat. Huntley and A.J. fell as well.

I tried to gasp for air, but none was coming. My lungs burned as liquid filled them. I struggled, trying to find a way out of this mess. *Had this been a mistake? Did these rings not work how I thought they did?*

The boat creaked as we spun out of control in Oceanus. I held on for dear life, wishing I could scream, but I knew that if I opened my mouth, more water would enter.

I got dizzy, the lack of air affecting me at last. The last thing I remembered was asking my father for forgiveness.

Chapter 8

Huntley

My eyes shot open, and I gasped for air. I choked on whatever water that was still in my lungs, and hacked it up and spat it out. Drowning, or almost drowning, was not fun. I didn't want to die again, especially since I had no idea what would happen. Mostly I just feared Tartarus. It was like the Krampus of the Underworld, something that should be feared by all. If I could get back to Earth, I wanted to tell people to fear Tartarus, but I would probably just be labeled as crazy. Again.

Pain shot from my shoulder, as the wound from Chrys' darkness was still fresh from the day before. Being thrashed around by the goo that made up the veil between worlds apparently didn't help. Go figure. I grasped it, hoping that would help. Nope, it made it worse. *Owww…*

Chrys was standing above me, her wet clothes clinging to her body. She should have picked a better bra because it was really hard not to look. I guess she had no idea that this was going to happen either.

She looked relieved as I started to get up. She let out a brief sigh. "Thank goodness you are all right. I didn't think you were going to wake up."

She glanced down at my shoulder. Shit, she could probably see it now. I was hoping that she would never see it, never remember what happened. It was fine, really. It wasn't her fault that she had so much power.

"Was that from me?" she whispered.

"Don't worry about it, it's fine." I coughed some more, as water was still in my lungs. Worse feeling ever. Worse than ODing by far. Well, maybe. It had been a while, and pain can fade with memory. Or at least physical pain could. "What happened?"

A.J. was sitting next to me, soaking wet as much as we were. He seemed bored, as if waiting for me to wake up was a nuisance. *Such a dick.* "We made it through Oceanus. We are on Earth."

I glanced around. We were next to some kind of river, the gondola sitting in the water, as if it didn't just transport us from Hell. Literally. There were some bridges and... "Holy shit, we are in London. That's Big Ben!"

Chrys glanced over, still frowning about finding out what she had done to my shoulder, but trying to act as if it was fine since she knew I didn't want to make a big deal about it. "Okay, that's what I thought, but wasn't sure. A.J. had no clue, he hasn't been on Earth for 4000 years and if I remember right, this clock hadn't been built yet."

I laughed. "No, no it hadn't." I couldn't believe we were in the city. The sun was just beginning to rise and, from what I could tell, Big Ben said it was half past seven in the morning. People were beginning to go about their day and no one noticed as we sat there completely wet with a gondola beside us.

Damn, I already loved this city.

"How did we end up here?" I asked. "Not that I'm complaining, this is great. I just don't understand…. of all the places."

"I think my mother was here last. The portal was probably already open and such," Chrys said as she sat down and we all watched the sun rise together.

I wasn't sure how she was taking all this, especially after seeing my shoulder. She sat there and fidgeted with her ring. A lot was probably going on in her mind as she thought about actually being on the Earth. I wondered if she thought it was worth it, going through Oceanus and disobeying Hades. Hell, I wasn't even sure it was worth it. London, though, from what I heard, was pretty awesome.

"Well, now what?" I asked.

Chrys shrugged. "I… I don't know. What does

one do here?"

"Yeah, this is a lot different from when I was on Earth. These buildings are massive, I can't even imagine how many thousands of men had to carry bricks and climb high to place them just so," A.J. commented.

I laughed. Finally, I had an advantage over him and was ready to rub it in his face. "No, there are machines that help. It doesn't take nearly that many men. Though I think first we should get some dry clothes."

Chrys snapped her fingers and all of our clothes were dry instantaneously.

"Why didn't you do that earlier?" I asked, especially since her shirt had been practically see through.

She shrugged. "Didn't think about it. Was too busy trying to get you to wake up."

Fair enough. I glanced around. I didn't know the city at all, other than from movies. "I guess we just explore the city. I've never been here."

"You haven't?" Chrys asked. "How far away is

your home then?"

I laughed. "Quite a ways. Over an entire ocean."

"Maybe we could visit it real quick?" she asked. She seemed genuinely interested in visiting my home. I didn't know why, it was a hellhole. It wasn't like this place, where we could have an adventure like no other. In my hometown, we could pretty much do drugs or go to the arcade. Or both.

I thought about explaining to her how difficult it was to get across the Atlantic to Philadelphia, but I decided not to go into it. "That's okay, I don't really want to scare people I knew. Besides, I've had enough water crossing adventures for a lifetime." That was a lie, I totally wanted to scare them, haunt them, it would be great. But I didn't want to waste my adventure on them.

She smiled a little bit. It was apparent she was still nervous about being away from the Underworld. Speaking of which, so was I. A.J. was the only one who was calm about the situation, which was weird. I grabbed her hand, reassuring her it would be alright.

"Should we go explore?" I asked.

"Yeah, let's."

We started down the walkways when Chrys finally caught sight of The London Eye. She pointed at it. "What is that? Is it a titan? Should we run?"

I laughed. "No, no, that is a Ferris Wheel. A really big one that lets people observe all of the city."

"Oh, people are *in* it?" She asked.

"Yup. Each of those little capsules have a few people in them."

A.J. studied it further. "How does it run though?"

"Oh, through electricity, mechanical engineering, I'm not completely sure since I didn't do that great in science... or any subject, really."

"Then why exactly are you Chrys' tutor?"

He had me there. I wasn't even sure myself. I glanced over at Chrys, who was still studying the London Eye skeptically. "So it's not actually an eye?" she asked.

"No, it's not. Just looks like one."

She nodded slowly, as if trying to take it all in. Then she pointed across the water. "What is that? Is it part of Olympus? Should we stay away from it?"

I laughed again. "No, it's a cathedral. St. Peter's I believe." Wow, I couldn't believe I had retained that information. Maybe it had been from tutoring Chrys, though most of that was helping her go through books.

"To worship a god?"

"Yes."

"What god?" A.J. asked. "My father, since it is near water?"

I shook my head. "No, a different god of a different religion. I would say we should stay away from it, as I never had one decent memory in a church, but at the same time I kind of want to take the daughter of Hades there…"

A.J. and Chrys just looked at me, confused by what I was trying to say. I let out a brief laugh. "Never mind, not important. Let's keep looking around."

We walked past the London Eye, around the bend of the River Thames. I kind of acted like I knew where I was going, but honestly I had no idea. Most of the things I knew were from T.V. shows.

"Whoa," Chrys said as she stopped on the sidewalk. Whatever nerves she had starting out were overshadowed by curiosity at this point. "That's the Globe Theatre!"

Of course she knew that. She looked so excited about it that it made me smile. I was glad she was enjoying herself now, especially after everything. I hoped that if Hades found out about our trip, that he would see that as well and wouldn't be too angry at us. Yeah, like that was going to happen. "What, was William Shakespeare a friend of yours?" I asked jokingly.

"He was a great mentor, for a short amount of time, anyway."

My jaw dropped. I mean, I knew people in history would have gone to the Underworld, sure, but didn't really think that she would know anyone so famous in history. Then again, I guess A.J. was some kind of king or something. He wasn't in any of my textbooks.

"He was your mentor? What did you learn from

him?" I asked.

She shrugged. "English, plays, history. It was fun, but then he went to Elysium like most of my mentors do."

Well I wouldn't. I didn't say that out loud, and was surprised that A.J. didn't either. Was I the only exception? Why did she even want me as a mentor, anyhow? Why did she even bother saving me?

She had mentioned souls drifting in the rivers in the Underworld if they had killed themselves. Was that where she found me? Was I one of those lost souls and she pitied me enough to sneak me into the palace and convince her father that I was something special? Someone that needed to stick around? If so, for what purpose? I mean, there had to be hundreds of souls out there roaming the Underworld, lost just like I had been. Why did she pick me?

It was something I wanted to ask her myself, but I decided not to. It could have been because I didn't want to know the answer, or just because I didn't want to put Chrys on the spot. I could ask A.J. but he probably would just lie, seizing the moment to make me feel bad. It was already apparent that he wished Chrys had never found me.

We kept moving down along the river, letting Chrys get an idea of what the city was like and what the wider world was like. A.J. and her were both amused with all the buildings, taller than anything they had ever imagined. When an airplane flew above us, I thought the two of them were about to have a heart attack.

"It's a god! What are we going to do? They are going to tell Zeus!" Chrys started panicking. I grabbed a hold of her.

"Breathe. It's an airplane. I told you about them, remember?"

She nodded slowly. "A bit. You said they could fly…"

"Yup, see? They fly. You're safe. Don't start to worry until you see me worry, okay? Otherwise we aren't going to get anywhere. You can ask questions, just don't cause a scene." Because seriously, people were staring. Not many though, because it was a bustling city after all. No one noticed each other in a city as they tried their best to ignore everything around them.

"Okay…"

"That goes for you as well, A.J."

He shrugged. "Wasn't scared."

Yeah, right. I thought about commenting but knew it would just lead to an argument. I didn't feel like arguing when we could be exploring this city instead.

There was so much to see, I didn't even know where to start. Though I guess I was better off than the two of them, as I knew what some things would be to do, whereas they had no clue. You would think after all the mentoring Chrys had, that she would know something about this place. Not really, it was a lot different probably than she had ever imagined. Then again, if I got thrown into Ancient Rome, I would only know a couple of places to go. I just wasn't used to it, and the culture differences were large. It was a wonder we got along so well.

"What's that place?" Chrys asked after a couple of hours of walking around, exploring.

I glanced over to where she was pointing. "The Tower of London. It's where a lot of the prisoners were thrown into during the Middle Ages through the Renaissance. Lots of death and famine are tied with this place."

Her eyes brightened at the idea of death. It was cute, but a little disturbing to say the least. I guess it was what she knew best, although as a human it was a little concerning.

"Can we go in?"

I rubbed my neck. I forgot about money. I had no idea how we were going to do anything here without that. "I think you have to pay to get in and we don't have money or ID's for that matter."

"What does the money look like now? And what is an ID?" she asked as she rubbed her hands together.

"Well, an ID is an identification card. I'm not a hundred percent sure what they look like in England, but for money all we need are little squares about this size." I motioned my hands in a small rectangle. "They would have our names on them and then numbers to a bank account."

A.J. pointed at a couple who were at the ticket booth. "Like those things?"

I nodded. "Yeah. Like those."

Chrys held up her hand and six cards appeared, three IDs and three credit cards. I grinned widely, forgetting that she could do that. "Oh, this is going to be a lot more fun than I could have ever imagined."

Chapter 9

Chrys

We went *everywhere*.

Seriously, I thought we had traveled all over the world, but apparently it still was only the London metro area. We had ventured through the Underground, which freaked me out because I thought we were going to where my dad was. Huntley assured me that we weren't going to the Underworld, that the Underground was a subway system, a way humans got around the city. It was scary, and I panicked a little while we moved, but I finally got the hang of it.

Now we were in Piccadilly, somewhere north of where the gondola waited for us. I felt weird being so far from it, but A.J. had said mortals wouldn't be able to see it.

There were people everywhere. I never imagined it would be this crowded in the mortal world. I mean, there were a lot of souls in the Underworld, but for some reason it never clicked that there would be so many bodies in one place.

There were moving vehicles, run by magic. Huntley tried to explain how they worked but gave up when I called it all magic. A.J. had the same look of surprise and fear as I did. It made me feel a bit better, as he always acted like he knew Earth better than I did.

This was as an eye-opening experience. I never imagined Earth to be like this and kind of understood why my mother liked it so much. I didn't think it was better than the Underworld though, nor did I think it was alright for her to act like the Underworld was the worst place in all the worlds. I could see one getting sick of things in this world, as Huntley said he was. He preferred the Underworld, or at least that's what he had told me.

I wondered what more we could see, and how much longer we would decide to stay here. I was already getting home sick and missed my puppy. I hoped he wouldn't give Father much trouble since I was going to be gone for a couple of days. Cerberus always worried when I was gone and wouldn't listen to Father very well. It was comical, especially since the dog has been around longer than me. Father probably trained it to be protective of me, and then it got out of hand.

Across from where we were, moving pictures with lights shifted color. I gasped as it seemed to be bigger than any painting I had ever seen, covering the entire corner of a building.

"What's that?" I asked as I pointed up. People around me looked at me like I was psychotic. Even a guy wearing a white shirt, puffy blue and white striped pants, along with long blue socks with black shoes gave me a suspicious look. He was one to stare.

"It's an advertising screen. Ignore it, everyone else does."

"How can you ignore that?" A.J. asked. "It's huge. It's bright. It has to have some magnificent purpose."

Huntley shook his head. "Nope. Just kinda there."

My eyes widened as I saw the statue in the middle of square. "Great Zeus, is that Eros?"

Huntley shrugged. "No idea, I'm not from here, not to mention I don't know who that is. Probably just a statue with no real purpose to the gods, just happened to pick one and went with it. It's really weird how different religions are used when it comes to art."

"Different religions?" I asked. I wasn't sure what he meant by that. Surely they didn't worship other gods above my father and his siblings. "I don't understand, do these humans not fear the gods of Olympus?"

Huntley laughed. "No, far from it. Only a handful of people in the world probably follow those gods.

Mostly everyone treats them as myth. No one actually thinks they exist."

I couldn't believe what I was hearing. After everything my father and his siblings have done for this world, everything they had built, yet they didn't think that we even *existed*. That was beyond rude and naïve. "How can they not believe in such gods? Who do they think brings a plentiful harvest, who do they think brings light during the day and darkness at night? Dreams and nightmares, rain and clouds?"

"I don't know, maybe Santa?"

I glanced at A.J. He shook his head, not understanding either. "Who is this 'Santa' and where can we find him? I recognize the name but can't quite place it. Doesn't he live somewhere north?"

Huntley rubbed his temples. "Never mind, forget I said that. Right now most people don't believe in a god, or they follow a different god. Rarely the Olympian gods. They have this thing called science and they believe that it answers all the questions of the universe."

I shook my head. "There is no way Urania could bless them with such knowledge."

Huntley shook his head this time. "Now it's my turn to be at a loss. Who's Uranus?"

"Urania," A.J. corrected.

"Whatever. Who is she?"

I answered, "she is the muse of science. She would be the one who would give humans the knowledge of science and inspire them. There is no way they would have meant to inspire them to turn their backs on us."

Huntley nodded. "That makes sense, actually. Kind of. Not really. Anyhow, now what do you want to do next?"

I bit my lip as I peered around. "I'm kind of hungry. What's good around here?"

A.J. nodded. "Yeah, I'm starving as well."

Huntley glanced around, then smiled. "Then we should dine just as the British dine. We shall find a tea house!"

* * *

I didn't know what afternoon tea entailed, but it looked delicious.

I watched as large trays went by with pots of tea and lots of desserts and sandwiches. Even my father would be amazed. I'm surprised he has never had this "afternoon tea" before, at least with me.

Huntley got us seats in the restaurant called Richoux. It was quaint, chandeliers hanging from the ceiling, with blue walls and red flowery wallpaper. I sat down, quiet, peering around, not quite sure what to expect. The waiter, a tall man with Viking orange hair, smiled as he stepped up to our table.

"What would you like to have?" he asked.

I looked at Huntley, not sure what to say. He turned to the man. "We will have the afternoon tea special. Earl Grey tea. All three of us."

The man nodded and took the clunky leather things off the table. They had the restaurant name on them, I wasn't quite sure what they were for.

"What did you order?" I asked. "Did you order one of those things?" I asked as I pointed at the three-tier platters.

He nodded. "Yup. That's what this city and country is known for. That and beer."

"Oh we should try that too," I said.

"Uh." He glanced at his ID card. "Yeah, I guess we can. The limit is 18 here, not 21 like it is where I was from."

"There is a limit to what? How much you can consume?" A.J. asked.

"Well, yeah, that too. But I was talking about age. Under a certain age, people aren't supposed to drink. When I died, I was only 16 and still five years under the age to buy alcohol," Huntley explained.

"Then how do you know it's good here?" A.J. asked.

"Just because I was underage doesn't mean I didn't drink. I just learned how not to get caught. Often, at least," Huntley explained.

A.J. appeared confused. "You disobeyed the king's orders?"

"We don't have a king, we have a democracy. The people voted to do it."

"Then why would you disobey?" he asked. I swore they got in the weirdest arguments. They weren't as bad as Mother and Father's arguments, but they were still pretty petty.

I missed my father, even though it had only been a few hours. I hoped he wasn't worried, and that he believed the note that we had left him. Although this was fun, I wasn't sure yet if it was worth it.

Huntley shrugged. "Because it's stupid. It's the majority voting for the minority, not to mention it means that a person can serve in a war but not be able to drink. It wasn't fair, so I didn't follow the rule."

"Anyway," I decided to intervene. I didn't need these two to start a fight in public. It would get out of hand fast and since we didn't fit in already, I didn't need more people staring at us. "We should try that later, then. But right now I am pretty excited about this."

The man brought over the pot of tea and three cups. Huntley said we had to wait for the tea to steep. Before the tea was ready, the waiter brought over the three-tier platter.

My mouth watered as I looked at the platter. There, in front of me, lay finger sandwiches of all different types, small scones with strawberry jam and some kind of white butter, fruit cake, and a pastry. All of it looked delicious, just waiting to be eaten. I couldn't believe that they had this every afternoon in Britain.

I picked up the cucumber sandwich and took a bite. It was delicious.

A.J. grabbed an egg salad sandwich and ate it quickly.

"Hey, you are supposed to savor it, A.J.," I commented.

"You know, I don't think I have ever seen you eat something so fast," Huntley laughed as he took a scone. Now that he mentioned it, I don't remember seeing A.J. eat something. That had to be wrong, he had to have eaten. But for some reason I couldn't picture it. There was no way. I probably just never noticed since it was never as outrageous as this.

Huntley poured us some tea after putting cream

and sugar in our cups. I waited a moment and took a sip.

It was *so* good. Better than any tea that I had in the Underworld. I tasted a hint of bergamot flavor in it. It wasn't too strong, nor too weak. I decided that when I got back that I would start playing around with different teas. I never realized they could taste this good. "Maybe I'll move here, this place is to die for."

"Ironically, it's quite the opposite, isn't it?" A.J. commented as he took another scone. "Humans die to go to your home and you wanna die to go where humans are."

I frowned. "It was just an expression. I didn't mean I wanted to leave the Underworld." I didn't realize what I had said. I loved my home, I wouldn't ever leave it to be here. I wouldn't leave my father to be all alone. It was just fun because Huntley and A.J. were there with me to keep me company. That and the rush of doing something forbidden.

I wasn't like my mother, I didn't hate it in the Underworld. I didn't want to cause Father pain like she did.

"I didn't mean it like that, Chrys." A.J. ate another scone. He was really hungry apparently. He must not have gotten something to eat before we left. "I just thought it was funny. I know you love your father and don't want to leave him alone."

"Yeah, this is just a vacation of sorts. One that no one knows about," Huntley added. "We will get back and it will all be fine. Everything will be just fine."

I nodded slowly and took a sip of my tea. He was right, this would all be fine. It was just a well-deserved break. Although I knew I should have waited to ask my father's permission before traveling to Earth, it was too late now. Sometimes it was easier to ask for forgiveness than permission, right? Didn't mean I felt okay about it though.

We finished the afternoon tea and headed back out into the city. As we stepped onto the sidewalk, Huntley clapped his hands together. "Now where to?"

I glanced around. There was a store right by us

that looked interesting. I pointed at it. "What's that place?"

He looked over. "Fortnum and Mason's. I've heard of it, I think it's a fancy store, where all the posh people go."

"Well, that's definitely not us. Let's find something more suitable to our liking."

Huntley laughed as he put his arm around my shoulder, guiding us towards where he thought we needed to go. A.J. followed, a little bit annoyed that Huntley, and I were getting along so well.

We found a punk store down the street, a tiny little shop with band shirts and jackets. I think I actually squealed when I found an Oomph! hoodie. They even had shirts for bands like Cute Is What We Aim For and Jack Off Jill. This is what I imagined Earth to be like, though it was just a tiny store in a back alley.

It was interesting to see how different humans could be. A.J. for instance didn't really like the music Huntley and I liked, nor did he care for the leather jackets and vests that they offered. I decided we should go somewhere after to shop for him, that way he wasn't wearing the same thing for the few days we were here.

I tried on a few jackets but decided I definitely wanted the Oomph! hoodie. It was one of my favorite bands, after all. As I put away the other two jackets, Huntley tried on a leather jacket and it made him look…

Sexy.

I bit my lip as he checked it out in the mirror. It fit him perfectly. It was definitely something he should keep and wear, like every day. He wrinkled his nose as he looked at it.

"Not sure." He turned to me. "What do you think?"

I straightened up, trying not to appear like I was gaping. "Looks fine. Up to you though."

"Buy it," the woman working at the store said. "She can't stop looking at you in it."

I blushed as Huntley smiled. "Well then, I guess I must."

I could feel my cheeks turning bright red now as

Huntley went to pay for my shirts and jacket, and his leather jacket. I couldn't believe she said that. But I shouldn't complain as that meant he would wear it more, knowing I thought it looked good on him. A.J. stepped up next to me.

"You really are interested in him, aren't you? He's just a punk human. He doesn't understand anything of what our world is like."

This was the first time we had this conversation in a long time. I wondered why he thought now was the appropriate time to talk about this. "That's not true. He understands."

A.J. let out a brief laugh. "As if. Hades only lets you keep him around because he makes you smile. You know he should have been left to roam the rivers until Charon found him."

"Is it a bad thing that I saved him? If he makes me smile, then why do you have a problem? I would say jealousy, but we both know that isn't the case. You had your chance, you didn't want me." I hadn't brought it up in centuries, as it wasn't that important. It was for the best if A.J. and I were just friends. But the way he hated Huntley, there had to have been something more to it.

"What, is he a replacement for me?"

I turned to him, frowning. "No, he's just something better that came along."

We both held each other's glare for a moment, until Huntley came with the bag full of clothes. He saw the tension between us two. "Uh… Did I miss something?"

The two of us shook our heads. "No."

"Okay…" Huntley pulled out two strands of knotted threads. "Chrys, I got us these."

"What are they?" I asked as he handed me the purple, white, and black one. He kept the red, black, and white one.

"They are friendship bracelets. You wear them on your wrist and don't take them off until the thread wears through. It's a symbol of our friendship."

I blushed. I couldn't believe he would get such a thing. He knotted mine around my left wrist, A.J. rolling his eyes.

"Here, now put mine on." I tied his together, and

he smiled. "Now we will always be friends."

I blushed and nodded. This was the best present anyone had ever given me and I had no idea how to express it. I stood there, silent.

"So then you two ready?" Huntley asked.

I nodded and smiled. "Yeah, we are."

We left the store, and I saw a group of teens walk by. They appeared to be the same age as Huntley, and the age A.J. and I appeared to be and were all wearing the same looking clothes.

"Why are they all dressed the same?" I asked. "Are they part of some kind of cult or following some type of god?"

Huntley laughed. "No, they are just in school. Though, to some people, that could be considered a cult."

I bit my lip, thinking it through. Schools were like tutoring, but with other people, all of them wanting to learn. At least, that's what I gathered. "What's a school like?"

"Horrible. Teens go to boring rooms where old people tell them how to think. There's a bunch of groups, cliques, it's awful."

I turned to him, smiling. "I wanna go! Take me to a school!"

Chapter 10

Huntley

Seriously? We were doing this?

We stood in some high school administration office; I had no idea what the school was called as I didn't want to be there. Chrys seriously wanted to see what a school was like. Out of all the things in London she could possibly see and do, this is what she wanted to do. I tried so hard to talk her out of it, but she insisted. A.J. didn't care, he was apparently just along for the ride.

I felt like banging my head against the wall. This

was so not what I wanted to do today. Or ever.

She thought her mom was a slut, just wait until she met some of these high school girls.

I had no idea how we were even going to get into the school. Our IDs said we were over eighteen, we didn't have any guardians, any residence in the area.

But then I remembered—she was a goddess.

She could apparently talk humans into doing anything here. It made me wonder if she ever used that power on me. Probably didn't ever need to, she was a pretty girl with a gorgeous smile, I would do anything she asked. That, and her father was Hades and could send me to Tartarus once he caught up with us.

Chrys smiled to the administration woman. "We would love to join this school. What do we need to do?"

The administration lady gave her a look. "It's not that simple, miss…?"

"Oh, my name is Chrys, short for Chrysanthemum."

I turned to her. I actually didn't know that was what her name was short for, she always went by Chrys. I let out a brief laugh. "Really?"

She narrowed her eyes at me. "Shut up."

"Well, miss Chrysanthemum, we don't just allow walk-ins. You must have residency, guardian signatures, and from what I can tell you aren't even the right age."

Chrys smiled. "Well then, I guess we will have to figure out something, huh?"

Chrys got her way. She changed our ages on the IDs and somehow convinced the lady that we lived there and that her parents had already come in to deal with the paperwork. There suddenly was paperwork on the table for all three of us. Amazing, she could use her power to get into lots of trouble, but instead she uses it to enroll in high school. Maybe I didn't rub off on her as much as I had thought.

It would only be for a couple of days, I knew, but it still wasn't how I wanted to use my time with

Chrys. London was a fun city, there were a lot of clubs we could hit up, but now our IDs said we were underage. I supposed that she could easily change them back so we could go at night.

As for A.J., he seemed relaxed about everything that was going on. I thought that this could bring attention to us, as Chrys had been using her powers out in the open, that if there were some kind of Greek god or nymph or whatever, they could see what she is doing and start questioning things. He said not to worry too much about it, that there weren't that many beings out there, and that a high school would be the last place they would look. I supposed he had a point, but it still made me worry.

Chrys appeared to be happy, though, and that was all I could ask for. She needed this to get her mind off of home and so I stopped fighting the idea of going back to school. This was a British school, it had to be better… right?

School wouldn't start until the next morning and we needed to find a place to stay. I knew this wouldn't be a problem as London was huge with a lot of hotels and hostels in the area. We would find something.

Wait, we had money. We could stay somewhere nice.

I looked forward to staying at a nice hotel. Seemed silly though, since I now lived in Hades' palace. Nothing could compare to that, but the idea of staying at a really nice hotel was always a dream of mine.

And then trash it.

I wasn't sure if I would actually trash it, as A.J. probably wouldn't let us. I knew Chrys would want to right before we left to go back to the Underworld. Mister "Do-Right" A.J. always cramped our style.

"What do I need for school? Do I need different clothes?" Chrys asked as she looked inside the bag.

I shook my head. "No, that school doesn't have a uniform or anything. We probably need some pens, a calculator, and a notebook to fit in. In the end we really don't need those things since we won't have to take tests or do homework."

"Where do we find those things?" A.J. asked.

I glanced around. "Not sure. An office store I guess. We will keep an eye out for one. Also, we need to find a place to stay. I was thinking a nice hotel since we don't have to worry about money."

Chrys shrugged. "I don't really know, is there a difference in places to sleep?"

I nodded. "Oh yeah. Just you wait."

We finally found a hotel that had a suite open with three bedrooms. I really was just asking for two, but A.J. insisted on three. He was a jackass.

The room, however, wouldn't be ready until another couple of hours. They let us leave the bags of clothes there, thankfully, as I didn't want to be carrying them all over London, and said they would put them in the room once it was clean. I thanked them, and then we headed back into the city, looking for more things to explore.

As we headed down the street, I spotted a ferris wheel. It had been such a long time since I had been to a carnival. "Hey, Chrys, look! There's a carnival. Do you want to check it out? They have a bunch of games and stuff."

She nodded. "Sure. That sounds like a lot of fun."

We started for where I saw the ferris wheel, and when we got closer, I realized it wasn't just a carnival.

It was Oktoberfest.

This day was just getting better and better. Chrys could change our IDs back to saying eighteen, we could drink a bunch of German beer, go on rides. This was going to be great.

"There are a lot of people here, are you sure this is a good idea?" A.J. asked.

I shook my head. "Oh, this is going to be the best idea ever. This is a festival the Germans created long ago, to kick back and relax after a plentiful harvest."

"Oh, so this is like a festival for my grandmother Demeter?" Chrys asked.

I shrugged. "Yeah, sure. Whatever. The point is to drink and be merry. Ready to have a good time?"

Chrys shook her head. "Of course."

Oktoberfest in London was a blast.

We went on all the rides at least twice. It was so much fun to see how loud Chrys could scream as the rollercoaster plummeted down, and how freaked out A.J. got on it was priceless. I will be poking fun at him for a long while.

Now, the beer was delicious. So much beer, oh my gods. We all got steins because that's what you do at Oktoberfest, right? I tried a couple of German beers and then a couple of English beers too. It was a lot of beer and I didn't think I could have so much at once and not feel that bad off. It must have been because I was the living dead or something. I wasn't quite sure how my body worked on Earth, if there was a body here and one buried wherever in the United States, if anyone even bothered. It was all rather confusing, and I tried not to think too much about it. Especially after alcohol.

Chrys, on the other hand, had lost count of how many beers she had. She was that little girl you didn't think could hold their liquor but really could and could out-drink most men. I didn't know if it was because she was a goddess or if it was simply her personality. I could see her mom getting drunk fast, one martini and she was dancing on the bar, although that might have nothing to do with alcohol. Her father, though, I could see being a silent drinker, one that you don't realize has drank five glasses of whiskey, yet could still be fine and outwit and fight anyone who dares cross them. Yeah, I had a feeling she took after her dad.

I could tell after the last one that she was starting to get tipsy, starting to slur her words. I decided that she better not have anymore, especially if we were going to go to school tomorrow. In fact, it was getting late, and I knew we would want a good night's rest after all that we drank.

Hm. That was a first that I thought about going to bed early after drinking. Was I becoming A.J.?

Chrys had definitely changed me, for the good I might add. Years ago, when I was alive, I would probably have stayed here until it closed, then gone to some kind of bar, got wasted, or even shot up with something I bought on the street. And god only knew whether I would have shown up to school the next day. I wasn't in a good place when I died, and lucky for me that I landed in the Underworld where Chrys was, instead of hell where a lot of people screamed at me saying that was where I was going.

Showed them, eh?

I wondered how long it would be before Chrys sends me on my way, sick of having me be her tutor, not that I really tutored her in much anyway. Sure I gave her information I knew, whether it be good or not, but most of it was from textbooks that she had found. She could have easily learned things straight out of them without my assistance. She was pretty smart after all.

But maybe she didn't just see me as a tutor, maybe she saw me as a friend. I had given her the friendship bracelet, but she didn't really say anything. Should I have not done that? She didn't seem to mind though, but I had put her on the spot.

A.J. had been in the palace since he died four thousand years ago. Maybe I would have the same chance as him, being her friend. Maybe even more...

No. That wouldn't happen. I was just a human, one that hadn't conquered a land or developed some kind of weird revolutionary thing. I was just some kid who grew up on the wrong side of town, hung out with the wrong people, and destroyed his life before he was even an adult. I wasn't anything special. There was no way she would ever want me.

As we walked out of the Oktoberfest, Chrys grabbed my hand and leaned her head on my shoulder. "That was a lot of fun, Huntley. I wish we could do the same thing in the Underworld."

She was being a lot more intimate now that we were out of the Underworld, and more importantly, away from her father. Maybe I did have a chance, but even so do I take it? If I wanted what was best for her, I knew that I shouldn't.

"Yeah, but there is a lot of other fun things you can do in the Underworld that you can't here."

She let out a slight laugh. "Oh yeah? Like what?"

I glanced over at A.J., wondering if he had any ideas. He gave me one of those, you dug the hole, get your own self out of it, looks. Such an ass.

"Helping the dead. There's only so much you can do on Earth to help people, but in the Underworld you have enough power to help the dead get where they need to go. When you are in power, I bet you will make sure there are a lot less lost souls out there, and that you will be compassionate and fair. That's the difference."

"I guess you have a point," she whispered. She stayed silent as we kept on towards our hotel. I flipped A.J. off where Chrys couldn't see.

"And, Huntley?"

"Yeah Chrys?"

She paused for a moment. "I'm sorry about your shoulder. I didn't realize I had hurt you."

I shook my head. "Don't worry about it, it's almost healed, anyway."

She made a little bit of a smile, but I could tell it wasn't real. She worried about hurting me, I knew. But it didn't matter, she couldn't stop me from trying to help. I wouldn't leave her, not for anything.

Chapter 11

Chrys

A loud bell rang, making me jump.

Huntley put his arm on my shoulder. "It's okay, those bells are there to tell us we have five minutes to get to class, then there will be another bell letting others know that they are tardy."

I nodded, as if I understood. I really didn't but I didn't want him to know that. I wanted to appear collected, as if I had this under control.

But in reality, I really didn't. There were teens everywhere, of all different types, as Huntley put it.

He pointed out the jocks, goths, punks, rich kids, cheerleaders, misfits, and others. I didn't know what any of those meant, how a word could define a person like that. I asked what we were considered, and he said it was complicated, but that A.J. could go sit at the jock's table during lunch and that he would fit right in. Whatever that meant amused Huntley, but left A.J. and I feeling confused.

Maybe this was a bad idea.

Huntley guided us to our first class, which apparently was a room where a grumpy old person yelled at students for an hour or so. It didn't sound like fun and I was confused as to why so many teens would take part in such a thing.

"Just roll with it, alright?" Huntley said as we sat at a table in the back. "Don't worry about seeming normal, if you are seen with me you will never seem normal."

I wasn't sure what he meant by that either, but as the other bell rang, which made A.J. and I both jump again, an older gentleman stepped into the classroom.

Teens all over were still loud, talking amongst friends, or sometimes enemies, Huntley said.

"That's enough. Settle down," the teacher said. I watched as people around us reluctantly turned their attention back on the teacher. Was he going to be like my mentors? He didn't seem so as he frowned, looking down on all of us. A mentor would never do that to me. Then again, he didn't know who I really was. "Good, now we will begin with going over Shakespeare. Open your textbooks to page three hundred and ninty-four."

I looked at Huntley urgently. He simply leaned over to another table and grabbed a guy's book. "Borrowing this, give it back at end of class."

The guy glared at him but didn't do anything to get his book back. I wondered how Huntley could do that and not get into trouble, or maybe he just didn't care. Either way, the three of us shared the book.

The class was so boring. Shakespeare was interesting, I knew, he had been my mentor. But this teacher made his work seem boring. It was remarkable that he could do it in such a manner, then get mad when students didn't understand. Yet, at the same time, he was degrading Shakespeare's great work. I thought about commenting on some of his wrongful ideas of the sonnets, but I doubted he would believe me. He seemed stubborn in his false ideas.

Next class was math, which was, well, math. That didn't change since it was the fundamental science. Then we had chemistry.

"Why are we wearing these things?" I asked as I put the goggles on. "They seem ridiculous."

Huntley nodded. "They are, but sometimes they are for safety. Apparently though, some kids are troublemakers and cause chaos. This is to protect those around the troublemakers."

A.J. sighed. "How come I have a feeling you were one of those troublemakers?"

I let out a little laugh as Huntley appeared to be hurt by AJ's snide comment. I thought it was cute when Huntley acted offended and innocent, though he knew he wasn't fooling anyone. Even with all the trouble he got into, or got away with, I knew he always meant well by it. Mostly he did it to make me smile. I wondered how long it would be until he was tired of doing such things for me and would want to leave for Elysian Fields, just like the others.

Huntley responded, "I would never ever cause trouble in a place as dangerous as this. There are chemicals everywhere. You know how bad someone could get hurt if someone did something they weren't supposed to?"

A.J. just shook his head, not believing his innocence. "What did you do in a class like this?"

"I may or may not have lit someone on fire. It was an accident, I swear, I didn't think his clothes would be that flammable with acetone on them, honest. But yeah, I got kicked out of the class for a whole year. It was fun."

"I don't think that would be my definition of fun," I commented. Even I was a bit afraid in here. I didn't want something to happen, not when I didn't know the rules of the bodies A.J. and Huntley possessed currently. It took me a while to get them breathing when we came out of the water, and if my hunch was correct, their bodies were mortal again.

Besides, I didn't come to school to get into trouble, I came to have fun. I came to see what life was like for humans. Then again, causing trouble was what life was like for Huntley before he came to the Underworld.

Huntley raised an eyebrow. Yup, he was a troublemaker. I had fallen for a troublemaker. Father would be so happy if he knew of Huntley's true nature, that was if he didn't put two and two together already. I didn't know what he would hate worse, if I did eventually decide to make him be my betrothed, the fact he was human or if he found out I had found his soul wandering the rivers in despair.

But that wouldn't happen because I wouldn't make Huntley have to endure the same eternal despair that my father has to endure being married to my mother. Their relationship was the only one I was ever exposed to, and if that was what marriage was truly like, I would take no part in it.

"Oh, yeah? Watch and learn." Huntley grabbed

one of the bottles from the table and sniffed it. Nodding, he poured a little on the table. "This is the stuff."

"What stuff?" I asked. I could smell it, barely. It was a little sweet and very strong.

"Magic." With that, he squeezed the flint, and a large flame engulfed the table. He simply laughed as A.J. and I jumped back, both falling to the ground. I had no idea Huntley could do such a thing. It was incredible.

"You three! Principal's office right now!" The teacher yelled.

Huntley put his hand to his head and saluted. Neither of us were sure as to why Huntley did that gesture, A.J. and I awkwardly saluted as we followed him out of the classroom. Apparently teachers were part military or something. Who would have known?

When we got out to the hallway, it was quiet, which was a large contrast to how it was earlier when we had ventured down it to class. I preferred it this way. It was much easier to travel now. A.J.

looked pissed, and once we were away from the door, he shoved Huntley. "What did you do that for, you idiot?"

Huntley pushed him back. "Because we are only here for a day. We might as well have fun."

A.J. shook his head. I was really surprised he didn't slap Huntley for touching him. I wasn't sure if he was warming up to him or if he hadn't even noticed as he was still glaring. "Is that what you did when you were human? You are despicable."

"Whatever," Huntley turned around. "You don't know what it's like nowadays. The world is so disorganized, everyone just needs to lighten up."

I wasn't sure what Huntley meant by that. He seemed to really hate being in this place, I started to regret forcing him to come to the school. I should have listened to him, but I was too preoccupied in seeing what humans did during the day. All of this was new to me, forbidden even. I only had this one chance to have hands on experience with the mortal realm and I didn't want to pass it up. But it definitely wasn't what I thought it was going to be like, anyway.

Huntley led us down the hall. Apparently he knew where we were supposed to be going. He said it wasn't his first time to the principal's office, but that still didn't answer how he knew where it was in this school. Did that mean all schools were constructed the same? I had so many questions, but I was afraid they were all repetitive and that I would only get on Huntley's nerves if I kept asking him these things. So I decided to only ask the important questions when need be.

We stopped in front of a door with half glass. There were a few chairs against the wall, one of them already occupied by a male student. He had brown hair, a soul patch, and had almost the same smug look that Huntley usually carried. He was probably a bit like Huntley, getting into trouble just as we did.

He looked us over. "What did you all do?"

A.J. glared at Huntley. "You mean what did he do? Started the table on fire with magic."

I elbowed A.J. He should have known it wasn't

really magic, but some kind of science. Then again, he hadn't been on Earth for four thousand years. A lot of stuff back then was magic to him.

The guy simply nodded, a bit confused, but didn't seem to care that A.J. had said 'magic'. "I see." He looked at me for a moment, his eyes sweeping up and down. I felt a bit self-conscious about what I was wearing. Maybe I should have worn something better? I didn't see anyone else wearing Oomph! hoodies, which I thought to be strange since they are the best band ever. "Haven't seen you around before, are you new?"

I answered. "I, uh, just came from out of town. First day." I tried to smile innocently. Apparently I was bad at lying. My father and Huntley were right. I just hoped my father wouldn't ask questions about where I was. I probably would break down sobbing and beg for his forgiveness.

"Ah, well, good luck. This high school is a bit hectic at times. But at least you made some good friends," he glanced at Huntley with a sarcastic smile.

Huntley appeared as if he were going to say something and start a fight, but I intervened. I didn't need a reason to get kicked out earlier than need be. "What about you, why are you sitting out here?"

"Oh, nothing much. Just argued with the teacher about a sonnet by Shakespeare. He was wrong on how Shakespeare was portraying love, but he also doesn't like being corrected."

I smiled. He understood as well. "I know, right? I noticed that during class too. He had it all wrong."

The guy laughed. He had a really good laugh, one that I could listen to over and over again. *Wait, what was I thinking?* I wasn't interested in him in any way, he just reminded me of Huntley a lot. Except instead of causing trouble, he was just arguing what was right.

Okay, maybe not *exactly* like Huntley.

"Glad I'm not the only one with more than half a brain." He held out his hand. "Name's Peter. What's your name?"

I shook his hand. "Chrys. This is Huntley and

A.J."

He glanced over at them, giving Huntley a little grin. "Well, I think you will fit in perfectly, Chrys. Not sure about your friend here, though."

Huntley held up two fingers and smiled. Peter nodded. "Yeah, also I'm not too sure if he is the kind of friend you want to make here."

"Well we are pretty good friends already," I said, holding down Huntley's arm as he was about to punch Peter again. I found it quite ironic, though, as both of them talked pretty close to the same manner, passive aggressively. Maybe that was why they didn't get along.

The door opened to the office, and a woman nodded to Peter. With a sigh, Peter stood up. "Well, see you around Chrys."

The door shut and Huntley stopped resisting me, pushing his arm down. "Why are you so nice to him? He's just a jerk."

A.J. sighed. "She's nice to everyone, you should know that by now."

I sort of resented that. Although my father was a

nice person, he was also known for being merciless if the time was right. I didn't want people always thinking I was nice and that they could get away with anything. Not if I wanted my father to take me seriously. "And he wasn't being a jerk, he was just making conversation," I added.

Huntley shook his head. "No, you don't know guys like that like I do. He's just a smooth talker, trying to get you to..." He sighed and leaned his head against the wall. "Never mind, doesn't matter. We aren't staying that long, anyway."

I wasn't sure what Huntley's problem was, but I decided not to ask. He didn't seem to want to talk about what his high school experience was like, at least not in any great detail. He mentioned hating it and the things he did, but that was about it.

After a bit, we were called into the office and Huntley got yelled at. He didn't seem to be even phased, as if he been through this all before. Luckily I was able to get the principal to calm down using some of my powers and let us go back to class. By the end of it, he completely forgot why we were called into his office in the first place.

By the time everything was finished, it was time for lunch. I was starving and could not wait to try high school food. We got into a massive line of teens all trying to get food. I figured it had to have been some of the best food in all the worlds for this many people to be lined up.

I was wrong. It was *disgusting*.

After a couple of bites, I felt like I was going to throw up. A.J. took my share, still hungry as ever. I swore he never ate this much in the Underworld. Once he and Huntley were done, the two of them took the trays to the garbage and tray stack. I sat there, waiting for them to come back. I kept an eye on them, kind of scared to be on my own in such a massive area, even though they weren't that far. I wasn't used to such crowds.

Most people just stayed away from us. I wasn't sure if it was because they didn't know us or if it had to do with Huntley's antagonistic aura. He gave off the 'step closer and get the fuck beat out of you' feeling and so most just stared at us like we were some kind of freaks. Huntley also pointed out that we didn't have British accents and that could be part of it. I honestly just think it was him.

But there was one person who would talk to me, and that was Peter. The boy I met in the hallway. He sat down next to me while A.J. and Huntley were still getting rid of the trays.

"Hi again." He smiled.

"Hey," I said, playing with my friendship bracelet. I wasn't sure why he sat down next to me, but I didn't mind since I didn't like being here all alone. Something about him seemed familiar, as if we were on the same level. My heart raced, as for just a moment I thought he could be some kind of god. That seemed highly unlikely though, as a god wouldn't hang out at a high school. That, and he didn't look familiar whatsoever. It was probably just because he reminded me of Huntley.

"I'm throwing a party tonight." He pulled out a piece of paper with an address and time on it. "Would love it if you could come. Everyone is going to be there. Don't need to bring anything except your beautiful self. Though you can bring your two friends if you want."

I nodded. "Okay, sure. I will see if they want to go." I didn't know what I was saying, I had no idea what an Earth party was like. Yet, for some reason, I really wanted to go.

He grinned. "Great. I will be waiting."

Peter left just as Huntley and A.J. showed back up. Huntley watched as Peter hurried off. "What did he want?"

I handed him the paper. "He is throwing a party. He said we were all invited."

Huntley looked at the piece of paper. "You can't be serious. Do you really want to go to this?"

I shrugged. That was the question, wasn't it? I wanted to see what life was like as a human, but the more I learned at this school, the more I came to realize that I missed my father and the Underworld. This wasn't me, I wasn't my mother. Although it had been fun yesterday, today I was starting to get sick of it all and just wanted to see the palace again.

"I don't know, I kind of do. How about this: we go

to the party, then we can go home. No more stops, just go straight back to the Underworld. What would you say to that?"

Huntley rubbed the back of his head. "I don't know, parties like this never end well."

I gave him one of my famous innocent smiles. "But you will be there with me, so it will be fun right?"

He glanced over at A.J. "Yeah, I suppose."

I bit my thumb. "What do you think I should wear? Should I get a dress or something?"

Huntley rolled his eyes at me as A.J. opened his mouth, but closed it before saying something.

It looked like I was going to get to go to my first party.

Chapter 12

Huntley

The day finally was over, thank God, or Zeus, or whatever.

I was glad this experience knocked some sense into Chrys and that she wanted to go back home after the party tonight. I would have preferred us not going to the party at all, but she insisted. For some reason she was really looking forward to it, as if she longed to go. Whatever, A.J. and I would be there and wouldn't leave her alone for any moment. Knowing that guy Peter invited her made me even more protective.

There was one more place Chrys wanted to stop before looking for a dress. And yes, she insisted that she wear a dress instead of something she picked up yesterday, as it was a party after all. Girls, I swore it didn't matter where they were from, Earth or the Underworld, they always wanted to look good at a party. I told her it didn't matter what she wore, that she was always beautiful, and although she did believe me, she still talked us into taking her to get a dress. Whatever. The fussiness women have overlooking nice for big events was something too hard to wrap my masculine mind around.

I also mentioned that she could snap her fingers and make any dress she wanted, but apparently that wasn't the same. She wanted the *whole* experience. I also asked her what she was going to tell her dad when he found all the clothes in her room. She didn't answer that, of course.

The last stop she wanted to make was at the British Museum. The history teacher today brought it up in class, and Chrys seemed very interested in seeing it firsthand. I couldn't blame her, especially since she could see relics of all the things that had come to pass while she was in the Underworld. It was odd to think that the girl I liked was alive for almost everything the museum had on display. And yet, she appeared only to be the same age as me.

Museums in Britain were cool. They were free, just a suggestion of a donation. Also, they were *huge*. Like I couldn't even comprehend how huge it was and how much stuff it had to have held. I wanted to say it held all the history in the world, as most of the artifacts were from different raids the British had during their empire days. It was a vast collection either way.

If my hometown had this, maybe I would have taken a liking to something at school. Or maybe not. Who knew, really, as it was because of Chrys that I started to take an interest in things.

We went through the different Asian cultures and relics that the museum had in store for us. Chrys appeared to be pretty interested in Muromachi art of Japan, along with their architectural style and zen-type decor. I had a feeling I knew what she was going to change her room into next. I wondered if she would like anime, and knew I had to introduce it to her when we got back.

A.J. liked the ancient middle east section, as there was a tiny plaque with his name on it. Apparently his full name was Agenor, Phoenician King of Tyre, but Chrys gave him the nickname A.J., as the "g" in "Agenor" sounded like a "j". I was hoping there was no mention of him anywhere, that way I could rub it in his face later. Oh well.

We came upon the Greek section. A lot of the art was inspired by Greek mythology, so Chrys was able to identify all of them and told me stories of who they were. It was great to see her so excited about it, even though she knew she could never be introduced to most of those gods and that none of them knew she existed. She had to stay hidden in the shadows, and although I knew it hurt her deep down, it didn't damage her to the point that she resented all of this. Because of that, I knew she was much stronger than I could ever be, even though at times her emotions would escape her control and she almost destroyed an entire section of the palace when that repressed fury erupted. Everyone had to have their faults, so I never held it against her. Besides, I doubted I could ever stand having no one think I existed, especially with so much power and so much responsibility. I knew she was lonely, but at that moment I realized just how lonely she really was. And I knew in my heart I would never let her stay alone.

We came upon a room with a bunch of statues in it. Chrys froze as she stared at one, a bronze figure of a woman. Slowly she stepped up to it.

I leaned over to A.J. "Who's that?"

"Her mother, you idiot."

Okay, now that he said that, I had to admit the statue did look a lot like Persephone. And Chrys. It looked *a lot* like Chrys.

Another man, probably in his late twenties, was studying the statue. As Chrys walked up to him, he glanced back between her and the statue. "Good lord, you look exactly like her! You must be a goddess!"

Chrys turned white. I wasn't sure if it was because she didn't want to be recognized as her mother, or if she was afraid somehow a god would find out. I quickly put my arm around her. "Yeah, my girl sure does look like a goddess, doesn't she?"

He gave me a look, realizing that I didn't like anyone trying to talk to her, especially guys who were apparently trying to hit on her. He walked over to another statue and acted like that one was more interesting.

Chrys sighed. "Thanks. Wasn't sure what was going to happen there. You are a life saver."

I beamed. "No problem. But glad that others can see how beautiful you are."

"I'm still going to go find a dress, Huntley."

Couldn't blame a boy for trying. I guess she was sticking to the dress.

"How come I don't see any statues of your father? I see plenty of Zeus and Poseidon," I asked. A.J. and Chrys gave me an annoyed look. Apparently I had said that a bit too loud as a couple of people were looking at us quite strangely.

She shrugged. "I don't know. Could be a couple of reasons. First off, my father isn't full of vanity like his brothers. Second, he doesn't leave the Underworld often, if at all, so not many humans know what he looks like, not until after they are dead that is."

"And the fact humans hate him because he represents death. Of all the gods, humans have resented him the most, fearing the afterlife and what it represents. They don't want to praise him because he sentences them to their death," A.J. added.

I never thought about it that way. I guess humans didn't really like thinking about death so it made sense, but having known Hades for a while, I knew he had to be one of the best gods out there, one that cared for humans more so than any that I knew. Then again, I didn't really know any others, only from stories. But he did make sure all the souls were judged rightfully, and he did so without bitterness, only with compassion. I knew I wouldn't be able to do it.

Chrys, on the other hand, would be next. She had the compassion, I knew, and could fight when the situation demanded it. I realized now that places like these, seeing all her family and other gods as mortal art forms, had to be hard on her. She would never see herself as a statue, never have anyone praise her for all that she will do. Hell, the world probably wouldn't even notice if she came to power, it would just go on being the way it was, totally ignorant of the immortal realms. I didn't know which I felt sorry for more, Hades for never being worshiped like the other gods, or Chrys for never being known like the others have at one point in recorded history.

Either way, it had to hurt.

"Why does your father always stay in the Underworld?" I asked, instantly regretting the decision. She already felt bad about leaving him there with her mother and coming on Earth without him knowing, even though it had only been a short amount of time since we left. She probably didn't want to talk about her father until we got back to the palace.

She shrugged. "Too busy, I suppose. He hates his brothers as well, so there's that. Not many really like him and a lot more fear him. He doesn't have many friends, so there isn't really a reason for him to leave. But mostly because he is too busy. There are always souls to be judged. Death never takes a break."

Made sense. Seemed like Hades got the short straw on this one though. It was no wonder he kept his daughter so close. He probably was pretty lonely. I mean, he had a few others who were down there, but none of them were really anyone you'd want to play poker with, or talk about the latest Underworld gossip. I mean, they weren't that lively.

Get it?

Well, I wouldn't let Chrys be lonely if I could help it. I knew that eternity was a very, very long time, but it was either eternity with her or an eternity wherever Hades decided to ultimately put me, which hopefully wouldn't be Tartarus. It really depended on how I treated his daughter. I just hoped I wouldn't do anything stupid, or get caught doing something stupid. Maybe this whole escapade to Earth might be counted against me in that way.

Knowing me…

"Is there anything else you want to see, Chrys? It's starting to get late and if you really want to get that dress, then we should probably leave soon," A.J. said.

She nodded. "Yeah, I'm done. Thanks Huntley for bringing us here. You have been a great tutor." She winked at me when she said tutor. I smiled as A.J. rolled his eyes.

"What, am I not good enough for you, A.J.?" I pushed him forward as we started for the exit. He gave me a sharp look.

"What did I say about touching me? And no, you are a worthless tutor."

"Yeah, well if it weren't for me, you two would be incredibly lost."

Chrys responded before A.J. could come up with some form of his trademark snarky response. "He has a point A.J.. If it weren't for him, we probably wouldn't have been able to come to Earth, at least not safely. The two of us would have been completely lost."

A.J. shut up and left the museum to help Chrys in her quest to go find 'the perfect dress'.

Okay, I finally understood why Chrys wanted to find a dress. And might I say *damn*, she looked so beautiful in the one she finally picked out. I knew it should have been obvious, but black was definitely her color.

She twirled around in her dress, a little black number that came above her knees. It was a bit like Belle's gown in *The Beauty and the Beast*, except not as elegant, and a bit nicer on the eyes to be honest. Not that cartoons could compare with the real thing. With the combat boots she was wearing, the way her hair was curled, and her dark makeup, she definitely looked like the princess of darkness.

And I wanted to kiss her *so* badly.

The fact we were away from her father should

have led me to believe I could get away with just one kiss. But A.J. was here, and he seemed like he would be a tattle-tale. Though he never mentioned the pomegranates to Hades, I think it was more for Chrys' sake than mine. If I stole a kiss, even if Chrys initiated it, Hades probably would still think it was my fault.

And down to Tartarus I would go.

I always thought fathers who were over protective of their daughters, saying they would shoot the boy who made their daughter cry, was absurd. First off, would they really shoot them? And second, they would get arrested if they did. Hades, on the other hand, could definitely cause an eternity of pain to whoever hurt his daughter. And he wouldn't face any repercussions. He was definitely the scariest father I had ever met. And, ironically, one of the nicest as well.

Chrys was still waiting for a verbal response from me as she stood in front of me, her hands on her hips. I must have been gawking this whole time, because she had a sly smirk on her face.

"Can't even come up with a response? It makes me look that sexy, eh?"

I glanced over at A.J. He was staring at her too. At least I wasn't the only one who was flabbergasted.

"Looks good," I said. "Really suits you."

"You think?" She looked at herself in the mirror again. "I'm not sure if I like the underskirt."

"Makes you look like a princess, but not so much as a sweet princess but as one who could kick someone's ass," I commented.

She laughed. "Fine then, this is the one I will buy."

Finally.

Chapter 13

Chrys

Now this is what I imagined Earth to be like.

There were teens everywhere, holding glass bottles, mingling with each other. Music by Schoolyard Heroes, if I was correct in my deductions, came blaring out of the speakers. I thought it was pretty good but it wasn't my favorite band, although this music set the party mode well at these mortal gatherings. I peered around in search of Peter, to tell him thank you for inviting me, but I couldn't pick him out of the crowd.

Huntley appeared tense, his eyes moving back and forth as he scanned the house for something unsafe. Always so damn vigilant. He kept close to me, not wanting me to step away from his view. I didn't mind; I liked having him around since he actually knew how to handle social situations on Earth.

Or at least knew more than me. The only social situations I knew were with my father, arguing with my mother, and hanging out with A.J. and Huntley.

A.J. kind of just tagged along. He seemed intrigued by the whole idea of the party, but wasn't sure what to expect just like me. He didn't seem to be amused or irritated, but more like he was deep in thought, as if thinking about something else. I wasn't sure as to what that "something else" could be, but I left him alone to mull it over on his own. As long as mulling didn't sour into brooding. A.J. was the kind of guy who just did what he wanted really.

We were going to leave Earth after this party, as I was starting to grow homesick. I missed my father and worried that he had found out I didn't go to Maka's place in the Underworld. If he did, he would probably ground me until the end of time. Though, then again, how was that any different from life before I left, I didn't know.

I recognized some people from the school earlier that day, but most of them I didn't have a clue who they were. I figured that they must be from the school, or other local schools, as no one here looked like they were older than eighteen.

"Hey cutie." A boy, probably a senior, approached me. He had curly blonde hair, blue eyes that looked me up and down. "Did it hurt when you fell from Heaven?"

I looked at him, confused and a bit worrisome. "I'm not from Olympus, but ascended from the Underworld. How did you know I wasn't from around here?"

The boy looked confused, his mouth open as if he were going to say something, but didn't.

Huntley grabbed me by the arm. "Don't waste your time."

I was confused by the whole conversation. "How did he—"

"He didn't, he was just trying to pick you up."

"Why would he want to pick me up? I'm perfectly capable of walking and standing."

Huntley sighed. "Don't worry about it. Just stay away from guys like that, okay?"

I nodded as if I understood, but honestly didn't. We went towards the open sliding glass doors that led out to the backyard. People were crammed into the room and didn't seem to care. It was a bit too much, if I was honest. It was worse than the hallways at the school. I couldn't wait to get back to the Underworld.

"This place is pretty large compared to many of the other buildings I have seen in London for living, am I correct?" I asked.

"Yeah, this is a nice place. Your *friend* must have a lot of money, or at least his parents or guardians or whatever," Huntley commented. I could see the distaste in his face.

"Why don't you like him? You don't even know

him."

He shrugged. "Because I have met a lot of guys like him, using their money to get what they want, picking on kids like me for living in a trailer-park, stealing girlfriends, starting rumors." He rubbed the back of his neck. "None of the kids in my high school were very nice or caring, especially when it came to me."

I didn't say anything in response. Whatever he went through had to have been hard for him, I couldn't imagine how anyone could be like that to such a nice guy. I was glad I found him and saved him from the river and that I was able to bring a smile to his face these past few years.

Every time I looked at Huntley, my heart began to quicken and my skin felt hot, especially seeing how protective he was over me. He knew the things that could happen in a school and didn't want anything that happened to him to happen to me in any way. I felt grateful and wondered why exactly he would do such a thing for me.

The time we have spent together here on Earth

made me realize how I really felt about him, how I wanted to be with him until the end of time, especially after his friendship bracelet gift. But he was a human, he didn't understand what eternity was really like, he didn't understand what the reality of being with someone for such a long time was—what it could do to a person. Sure, either way, his soul would last forever in the Underworld, just as I would. But it was different, being in the palace instead of paradise. It was a lot more... confined.

Even though I knew I wanted him, knew I wanted to be with him, I wouldn't let my selfish desires allow him to fall to the fate of being my boyfriend or partner for eternity. I didn't want anyone to face that fate, didn't want them to be in a loveless relationship like my parents and fight with each other for the rest of eternity. I had seen what so much time could do to a couple and I could never bring so much pain to Huntley. That was why I knew I shouldn't grab him by the collar and kiss those beautiful lips of his.

I once felt something for A.J., but that was a long

time ago. I didn't harbor any more feelings for him, but more just liked to be in his company, mostly out of loneliness. I preferred Huntley by far to be around, but A.J. had been a great friend for such a long time, I wouldn't ever turn my back on him.

I looked up at the sky. It was dark out, the sky lit by stars and the haze of city lights. I could barely see the stars, but I could tell that they were there. They were as beautiful as I imagined, but still not as beautiful as the River Styx. I missed home so much, I just wanted to go back.

But I told Peter that I would come to this party and learn what a human party was like. It was interesting to see what the different people were doing, but not as fun as I had imagined.

"Hey Huntley, I'm kind of thirsty," I said.

He glanced around. "I will go see what they have. You stay here with A.J. okay?" He turned to A.J. "And you, you don't let her out of your sight."

A.J. smiled sarcastically. "Yes, sir."

Huntley rolled his eyes and turned towards the rest of the home. I glanced around at all the people in here. It was quite crowded now, more and more people showing up. Almost everyone seemed to have a glass of beer. If this was mostly kids from the school, wouldn't most of this be illegal? Would police show up and arrest them? Was that threat really worth it? Everyone around seemed to think so.

I turned to A.J. who was also studying the crowd. He didn't seem to really care, though, as if just waiting for Huntley to get back. He seemed passive about everything on Earth, sort of just going along for the ride. He didn't seem to be interested in any of the things Huntley and I wanted to do, yet he went ahead and did them. In the Underworld, this wouldn't have been the case, but in fact he would have protested and made a fuss, or just leave and do his own thing. Something was going on with him and I wasn't sure as to what.

"So, what do you think of this place? Was it worth it?" I asked. It had been a while since I had talked to A.J., just the two of us.

He shrugged. "Definitely has changed, but the

overall feeling of Earth is still the same as I remembered it."

"Oh, and what feeling is that?"

"Freedom."

So that's what it was. He felt free here compared to the Underworld. I couldn't blame him, I felt almost the same way. The Underworld, the places we could go, wasn't that large. This city was larger than the places we normally ventured in the Underworld. Granted that there were three other parts of the Underworld that one couldn't go to without never coming back. From what I could tell, those places were endless, defying space and time. But A.J. hadn't wanted to go there. "You know Father will send you to Elysian Fields. If you want more space, why don't you just go there?"

He let out a laugh. "You think that space is the only thing that represents freedom? You are greatly mistaken."

"I—" I began, but suddenly Huntley appeared next to us. "Oh, Huntley, you're already back? Where are the drinks?"

Huntley stepped closer, staring back and forth between my eyes and lips. *What was he doing?*

He placed his hand on the back of my neck and pulled me closer to kiss. My first instinct was to push him back, knowing Father would never accept this. But Father wasn't here, he would never know.

I fell in the kiss as it deepened. I wrapped my own arms around Huntley, never wanting to separate.

"I'm going to go... Yeah, anywhere away from here." I heard A.J. comment, leaving us be. It was probably a good choice for him.

Huntley bit at my lip, his kisses becoming rougher. I had no idea where this sudden wish to kiss me came from and couldn't believe it at first. But after all this time, I always felt like something could spark between us, I just was never sure if he had felt the same way about me. Now I knew.

Being exposed in public like this, I am surprised no one tried to stop us, but then I remembered that most of the surrounding people were either drunk or also making out with someone. Huntley probably figured that since this was part of our last moments on Earth, why not? I had even been thinking about it for a while, but knew that if he didn't feel the same way, that it could have hurt our friendship in the process.

Thank goodness my father wasn't anywhere near here. I swore he had some kind of radar that made him step in at the most inopportune time. I had almost kissed Huntley a couple of times in my room, but he always walked in. Huntley could move fast by the way, but I guess when you were afraid of what the God of the Underworld could do, it made you be on the alert at all times. I always thought it was pretty funny, although annoying since this was the first time we actually kissed. I had feelings for Huntley the moment I first pulled him out of the water. Something just made me instantly fall in love with him and the more I got to know him, the more I knew I wanted to keep him in my life forever.

But was that what he himself wanted?

Humans were fickle beings. At least that was what my father always said. That was why I went through tutors so fast. They would get sick of teaching me and want their reward. It was always my biggest worry that Huntley would grow bored with me, that he would leave eventually. But that didn't matter right now. What mattered was I could get away with doing the things I wanted to him without my father knowing.

Huntley's lips moved to the side of my mouth, to my cheek, and down my neck. I took a deep breath, wanting so much more. Slowly he pulled me back, stepping towards the stairwell.

Chapter 14

Huntley

Where the hell the kitchen was with the drinks, I had no clue.

You would think it would be easy to find the drinks in this place, just follow where people were gravitating towards with empty beer glasses in hand. But no, it had to be harder than that. The drinks apparently had to be hidden so that it would take forever for people like me to find them. Not to mention my shoulder was sore. Stupid shoulder.

It was annoying to know what life was really like

for students like these. The drugs, the alcohol, the self-inflicted wounds. It brought back many memories that I didn't want to face, that I didn't want to ever think about. I had found Chrys and that brought me out of the darkness. Or maybe into the darkness since her father was Hades. Either way, I was happy now, and I didn't need these things to make the pain go away. I had her.

I wished I was brave enough to tell Chrys that, to tell her what my life had really been like on Earth. I knew she understood that it was hard, and she never pressed further about anything. I loved that about her; I loved how she understood enough to know what to say and when to say it, yet at the same time didn't take any crap from anyone. Especially her mother.

I can't believe that all of this was because of how upset Chrys was with her mother. A.J. had talked her into coming to Earth, seeing what her mother had loved so much. Now that she was here for a couple days, she was missing her home, I could tell. This life wasn't for her.

Thank God, or Zeus, or whatever.

I didn't want to be back here. I liked it better in the Underworld, where we were (mostly) happy and having fun. Although Persephone could be annoying, it was easy to ignore her for the most part, Chrys knew that. She just had to have been dealing with it for so long that she couldn't take it any longer.

I thought about asking someone where the beer was, but I didn't want to get laughed at, or be called such a stupid American or something. I didn't know what exactly they would say, but I knew it wouldn't be nice. It never was. It was why I never trusted anyone, not until I met Chrys and her dad. I trusted him as well, as he had no reason to lie. He was very forthright in what he said. He didn't have anything to compensate for.

I finally found where the drinks were. They were in the garage, and here I didn't think there was even a garage in this house. That guy Peter must have a rich family in order to have such a big place. I wondered why he didn't go to a private school instead of the public one we pretty much crashed today. I couldn't believe that I had snuck into a school willingly. Usually it was the other way around, usually I was sneaking out of school. And getting caught in the process.

Though most of the time it was because I *wanted* to get caught. I liked it when the teachers or administration were mad at me, when my parents looked at me with such clear disappointment. It gave them a reason to hate me, an actual reason to hit me. It was better than getting hit and not having done anything so, I figured, since I was already getting the punishment, I might as well act out to deserve it. It was the only way I rationalized it to myself. That they wanted me to act out.

It kind of put me into a spot though, as no one believed me when I said that they abused me. People thought I was overreacting, as if being a punk kid meant I had no rights. That was how I felt, as if society cast me down and blamed me for everything. Look at how he dresses, he deserves to be mocked. Look at the way he stands, he deserves to be disciplined. Has an attitude problem? Well, those beatings must bring him some good. He had it coming. It was a vicious cycle that had no end. Although I knew I could have made better choices, I knew that it wasn't all my fault. That I had just gotten a bad hand of cards.

But that was in the past. Now I had a better life, or death I guess, and I would never let such a life happen to Chrys. I understood she needed to run away temporarily, but we had to do so without getting caught. It wasn't like in the past when I wanted to be caught, when I wanted to cause trouble. Chrys didn't want Hades to hate her, she just wanted to understand what it was like outside of the Underworld. In some sense, she wanted to know what motivated her mother to escape here, and even why I resented my life here.

So that's why I made sure she stayed safe, and why I didn't like leaving her out of my sight. She didn't face being abused by her parents, although some would argue what her mother did was abuse, and making her stay within the palace as well. But I was more afraid of what high schoolers would do. A lot of people saw kids and teens as being innocent. That was never the case, at least none that I had ever met.

A.J. was with her right now, so I knew she would be fine, and the fact it would only be for a brief moment.

I grabbed three beers, and as I turned to head back to where A.J. and Chrys were, I found A.J. was standing in the doorway. I about dropped the beers. Chrys wasn't with him.

"Where the hell is Chrys?" I asked, trying my best not to start a scene. I didn't need more people thinking something was up, not that these kind of people would be a threat to us. Nevertheless, I didn't want them to stare. I hated it when they stared.

A.J. looked back at where he came from, nervously. "She... You... I don't—"

"Spit it out, A.J.!" I yelled a little louder than I had wanted. Chrys wasn't protected now, she could be anywhere. See, this was why I didn't trust people.

Okay, for the record, I knew Chrys could take care of herself. She was the daughter of Hades, for crying out loud. But between knowing what humans were like and not wanting her to experience anything I had gone through. And the fact she couldn't get caught by other gods, I was just under a lot of stress and wanted to go back home. To the Underworld.

Huh. I considered the Underworld my home. Strange thought.

"You came and started making out with her! I came looking for a drink since you didn't bring anything with you." He looked at the three bottles. "But if you're here, then..."

I dropped the drinks, and we both ran towards where Chrys was. She wasn't there.

"Fuck!" I wanted to punch something, but there wasn't anything I could punch without getting in trouble for breaking it. But then again, would it really matter?

"We have to find her fast," A.J. said.

"No shit. What could have taken her? What can change its appearance to look like me?" I asked as I glanced around.

A.J. didn't respond at first, but his face became cold. "A lot of things. We need to hurry."

I prayed she was still in the house. London was too large to search everywhere. It wasn't like we could alert the police if she was really missing either. She wasn't exactly from around here, or anywhere on Earth. And she might not even be on Earth anymore.

I took a deep breath. "Ok we will split up and find her. Let's go."

A.J. and I turned our backs at each other and went in opposite directions. She had to have still been here, as the front door was close to where the drinks were and A.J. would have seen her leave. So my doppelgänger and Chrys had to be here somewhere.

It had gotten more crowded in the past few minutes, making it harder to move around and search. I wanted to punch most of these people in the face for not getting out of my way as I tried to get past them, but that would make it harder to search.

My heart was racing and sweat began to pour off of my skin. I could barely breath but had to focus. I had never been so afraid in my entire life, and death. I couldn't even imagine what would happen if I couldn't find her. What we would have to do? Would we have to go tell Hades his daughter was missing? God, I didn't want to give him that news. It wasn't just fear of what he would do to me, but more I didn't want Chrys to really go missing for that much time. I had to find her and make sure she was safe.

I searched throughout the entire first floor. I didn't see any trace of Chrys. I asked around, but everyone shrugged. I should have figured since no one ever paid much attention to anything but themselves. I cursed, for ever being a selfish human like them.

So far there was no sign of her and my heart wouldn't slow down. I had to find her before it was too late.

Chapter 15

Chrys

Huntley pulled me into one of the rooms on the top of the third floor and closed the door, his lips never leaving mine. They were warm, tasting like whiskey. He must have found a drink before coming back somehow. He had only been gone for a very brief moment. It seemed nearly impossible, the more I thought about it. But I didn't care, I had been wanting him to kiss me for so long.

The only thing that had been holding me back was my father. Although he didn't mind Huntley, that didn't mean he would have ever approved of us being together, the argument mother and him had about my love life a couple of weeks ago proved that. Though I doubted anyone was good enough for me by his strict standards. It wasn't like I could really meet anyone else that wasn't in the Underworld either, so that left no love in my life, or at least in my father's eyes.

But now he wasn't here and I could do whatever I wanted with Huntley.

His lips were warm, as were his hands as they started to lift up the back of my shirt. I desired him so much, wanted him to grab me like this. Whatever had gotten into him all of a sudden, the realization this could be our only chance before we were back in my father's domain, I'm not sure. All I knew was I wanted him right then and there, my yearning for him taking hold of my body.

He pushed me up against the wall, his kisses harder, more demanding. I wanted more than anything to have the pomegranate seeds with us, to experience the most out of this, but nevertheless, they didn't exist here like they did in the Underworld. Besides, having Huntley like this was more than enough.

I grabbed on to his shoulder, then realized it was where I had hurt him the other day. "Oh, sorry. I didn't mean…" That's when I noticed that the wound was gone. "Huntley, what happened to…"

"What is it?" he whispered as he kissed my neck.

"Your wound, it's gone," I whispered.

Huntley pulled me back from the wall, laughing a little as he stopped kissing me. I looked at him curiously. "What's funny?"

He shrugged. "Just, with so much passion, so much longing, I thought you would have noticed."

I shook my head. I had no idea what Huntley was talking about. "I don't understand. What are you talking about? What happened with the wound? Last time it took over a week—"

Huntley waved his hand in front of his face. It molded into another, into the boy that had invited me to this party.

"Peter? How? What?" I didn't understand. how

could he change like that? Humans couldn't do that, could they?

Unless...

He bowed. "I am Pothos, an erotes of Aphrodite. The representation of longing and yearning, and boy do you yearn for that human. And why is that? You know he can never be like us."

My head felt like it was spinning. I didn't understand what was going on, how he was able to look like Huntley for a moment, and then return to his normal self for another. I had heard of the erotes, part of Aphrodite's posy. What was one of them doing here? This couldn't be happening. What was going on? How could he do that? "I still don't..."

"I can turn into whatever you long for," he said as he turned back into Huntley. He traced his fingers against my sides, pulling me closely. "And do whatever you yearn for."

I tried to push him away, but he was a bit stronger physically than me. If I had any doubt, he was one of the erotes, it was gone now. But it still didn't answer what he was doing here. "Get off of me you pig!"

"But you want this so badly," he whispered into my ear. "It may be your only chance." He kissed my neck, still appearing as Huntley.

The power shot out through my body in an instant, throwing him back against the wall. I was surprised he didn't go through it as my anger kept on rising. The air swirled around me, darkness and light gathering into it. I could feel raw energy resonating through my skin. I tried to control it like Father had taught me, but fury ran through my veins. I had been deceived. My feelings had been used up, and I would not stand for that. Not when it could mean Father finding out what I did, or any of the gods finding out I existed. All because some erotes wanted to play a trick on me.

"Wait!" Pothos held out his hands, turning back into himself. Any attraction I had towards him was long gone, though now I realized it was because he was connected to Aphrodite. I couldn't believe I had thought he was anything like Huntley. Huntley would never do something like this. "I'm not going to hurt you, I just wanted to know who you are!"

Yeah, like that made sense. Huntley had been right about him, I should have listened. Although Huntley thought he was human and was afraid of what a human boy wanted from me. Apparently human men and gods all acted the same. They just tried to use each other in the same manipulative way when they wanted something. They didn't care who got deceived or hurt in the process. All that mattered was them. I began to understand why my father didn't want me to leave. And why my mother fit in so perfectly with the rest of them.

"Then why didn't you ask? Why didn't you just say that from the start!" I exclaimed. He seriously messed with the wrong goddess.

He nodded quickly. "I know, I know. I'm sorry, I won't do it again. Just calm down! We don't want to make a scene!"

A scene? Please, he didn't know the meaning of that word. He was lucky he was still alive at this very minute. If my father was here, he would have destroyed this boy in an instant. Heck, he would have destroyed him even if he thought it was Huntley. "Why the fuck should I listen to you!"

"Because if I'm right, then everyone will know you are Hades' daughter!"

Everything felt as if it had stopped. The items that had been swooped up in my power simply fell out of the air and landed on the ground. All my power seemed to go away, as if he had just slapped me. Which he did, with the truth. "How do you know that?" I whispered.

He stood up, taking a few deep breaths and rubbed his shoulder. I didn't feel bad that he had hit it so hard against the wall. He deserved it. "Because I can see what you long for and why you long for it. You love Huntley, but your father is stopping you from doing anything about it. Hades is stopping you. And you smell like someone I know…"

I didn't say anything but just stared at him. My secret was out, I had ruined everything by coming to Earth. I shouldn't have come, I shouldn't have risked everything my father had done for me to see what Earth was like. I should have stayed in the palace. I should have just kept on ignoring my mother and stayed with Huntley and A.J. I ruined everything.

I sat down on the bed. "Then Zeus knows and I am dead," I whispered.

Pothos took a couple more deep breaths and messaged his shoulder. "No, no, no. I wouldn't tell that asshole. He doesn't know, or at least if he did it wasn't from me. I didn't tell anyone, I just wanted to learn more, to get to know who you really are."

I gave him a look. "By tricking me into sleeping with you?"

He gave a half grin. "It's not like every day you get a chance to sleep with Hades' daughter."

I punched him. Straight in the nose. He crumbled down on his knees. Huntley and Father would have been proud.

"Ow…"

"You deserved it, you asshole. Did you really just see me as a conquest? That was all you wanted to know about me? My *body*? You are *so* lucky my father isn't here." Seriously, what was he thinking?

Maybe I should listen to Huntley more. He seemed to hint at the fact that something like this would happen. Though, how he knew, I didn't know.

"So then he really is your father? That's…"

"Complicated? I know. But as for now, how do I know you are going to keep my secret?" I tapped my finger on my chin. "What could the daughter of the God of the Underworld do to make sure someone keeps her secret?"

"I swear to you that I would never cross Hades. *Never.*"

I raised an eyebrow. "Yet you would try to sleep with his daughter?"

He thought for a moment. "Point taken. I didn't think it through, but as for crossing him, giving someone his secret, that I would *never* do. I know the things Hades has done to people who have crossed him. I'm not going to let that happen to me."

I had reason to believe him. I knew how much my father was feared by humans and gods alike. I really doubted this god was lying. But then again, it seemed that he more feared Zeus than my father. "Fine. But you should know I— "

Suddenly, out of nowhere, glass exploded from the window. I put out my hand, making the glass bounce off of the invisible shield I had quickly created, something I had learned to do from my father. Came in handy when Mother got really drunk. Pothos had hid behind me.

From the broken window stepped a red-haired woman. She appeared the same age as me, somewhere in her late teens-early twenties, but something about her made me feel like she was much older, just like me.

"Oh fuck," Pothos commented to me. "Speak of the devil."

"Pothos, you aren't cheating on me are you?" She gave me a once over. "Hello, sweetie, let me introduce myself. I am Melinoe, the daughter of Persephone and Hades."

Chapter 16

Huntley

There was a loud crash at the top of the stairs coming from one of the rooms. I quickly ran up to the third floor to see what the commotion was. A.J. followed right behind me. We both knew it had to be Chrys. There was no way it couldn't have been. She probably figured out someone had tricked her and had let her emotions get the upper-hand. And if that was indeed the case, this whole house was going to get destroyed in the process.

So we had to act fast.

I almost tripped going up the stairs because I was running and had lost my footing. I cursed under my breath. Damn shoulder, why has thou forsaken me? Pain shot through my arm to the point where my hand felt numb. I did not want to deal with this right now.

We got to the top of the stairs and I was practically out of breath, as I had been running frantically through the room searching for Chrys. With my heart pounding and sweat dripping off of my skin, I quickly opened the door.

And I'm not quite sure what kind of scene I had just walked into. By the look on A.J.'s face, I'm sure he was thinking the same things I was.

What the fuck?

Chrys was fine. She looked shaken up a bit, scared, concerned, but she was fine. That was the most important thing. Peter looked like he had been hit a few times by stuff that had been thrown around the room. I knew it was Peter that was behind it. Well, I wasn't sure he was the cause of all this, but I hadn't seen him around when we were downstairs. It was his party, after all. But more interestingly enough, both of them stared at the red-headed girl that stood by the broken patio door. And by the looks of it, she appeared angry.

I hurried to Chrys' side. "Are you okay? Did he hurt you? Do I need to teach him a lesson? Because I will, so help me—"

She wrapped her arms around me. "I'm okay. But..." She looked at the red head staring at Peter. "She said she is the daughter of Hades and Persephone."

I turned and looked at her. I could definitely see the resemblance of Persephone, but I couldn't see any characteristics of Hades in her, and it wouldn't have surprised me if Persephone had more kids that she didn't tell neither Hades nor Chrys about. In fact, I kind of suspected it.

Peter shook his head. "Your father isn't Hades and you know that. It's Zeus. He disguised himself as Hades and had his way with your mother, just as he does with every other woman throughout all the worlds."

"You mean like what you tried to do with me?" Chrys shot back.

"*What*?" I asked. I wanted to know exactly what this creep tried to do to Chrys so I could beat the shit out of him. I promised her that I would keep her safe and I would. If I failed, I would never forgive myself. So if I had to beat the shit out of this guy, I would. I wished I could tell Hades as well because he could do even more things than I was capable of. But then he would also do those things to me since I had let his daughter leave the Underworld.

She nodded over at Peter. "He isn't human. He is Pothos, an erotes of Aphrodite. He disguised himself as you to get closer to me. A.J. was there, he can tell you."

A.J. nodded. "Yeah, I thought it was you, Pothos. I wasn't entirely sure, but it made sense. Huntley doesn't have the balls to kiss Chrys like that."

I glared at him, whether it was because he let this jackass kiss Chrys or because he said I didn't have the balls to kiss Chrys myself, I wasn't sure, but before I could say anything, the other daughter of Persephone spoke up. "And for that, Pothos, you will endure my wrath!"

He held up his hands. "Wait! We aren't dating anymore! You broke up with me! For Prometheus, of all people! He isn't even a god, he's a stupid Titan from before—"

"I don't care!" she spat out. "You still used me, you still shouldn't have broken your promise with me."

So she was one of those girls, one who cheated on their boyfriends, or broke up with them, then freaked out if they moved on. Or just didn't listen to them when they said it was over. Typical.

I mumbled under my breath. "Psycho-hose beast."

I thought I had been quiet about muttering that. Apparently I wasn't as she quickly turned to me. "What was that, *human*?"

Right, don't piss off the mad goddess. I needed to remember that.

I shook my head. "Nothing. Go on, have your

godly argument. But who exactly are you?"

"I am Melinoe, Goddess of Nightmares and Madness."

Oh great, that's all we need. I was about to reply because, seriously, we needed to get back to the Underworld, when the door opened behind us. It was another man, who looked to be about in his mid-thirties, ginger hair poked out of the hat he was wearing and scruff covered his face. His green eyes widened in surprise when he saw all of us. Apparently he didn't expect this scene either.

"Melinoe, what in Olympus are you doing here?" the man exclaimed.

Her eyes brightened, and the dark aura that had been surrounding her before vanished. Now she just looked like any ordinary girl. Love-struck, might I add. Yup, definitely one of those girls.

"Prometheus. I've been looking for you everywhere." She ran into his arms, almost as if she was about to cry, as if we had caused her so much turmoil. "I missed you so much. You haven't called me, I thought Zeus may have locked you away again."

I couldn't read Prometheus's face, whether he actually wanted to see Melinoe or if he had been running away from her. I presumed the latter from what I had witnessed so far. There was no way he could *actually* like her. There had to have been something more to it. Being the Goddess of Nightmares and Madness, I could only imagine what she was like in bed. There probably was a reason these two had kept her around for as long as they did.

Also, he looked much older than her. She appeared to be in her teens and he had to have been late thirties, early forties. I mean, it probably didn't mean anything to gods, but Peter, or Pothos, had said he was a titan. What exactly that meant, I had no idea. Maybe he really was a lot older?

"I missed you too, Melinoe. I was just about to call you. You know I'm in constant hiding, that if Zeus sees me, he could easily lock me up again just for the heck of it. I had to cut all ties this time, just in case that did happen."

Smooth one. I bet he was really just hiding from her. Because, let's face it, she seemed psychotic. Then again, it did seem like a lot of people wanted to hide from Zeus.

Prometheus hugged her, then glanced up at the rest of us. "Pothos, what are you doing up here? And who are you lot?"

Melinoe nodded towards Chrys. "He was trying to sleep with this *whore*, what does it look like?"

Prometheus took a look at the three of us. He didn't seem very impressed. As his eyes hovered over A.J., he squinted his eyes, as if trying to remember. "Agenor, son of Poseidon, is that you?"

A.J. nodded, looking a bit smug he was recognized for once. "It is. Long time no see, eh Prometheus?"

He shook his head in disbelief. "How are you here? How are you alive? It isn't possible—"

Pothos stood up, groaning. Chrys probably gave him that bloody nose. Good for her. "That girl is the *real* daughter of Hades and Persephone. She probably brought the two of them up from the

Underworld."

Seriously? He figured it out? And decided to tell this guy?

Prometheus looked as if he had seen a ghost. He stared at Chrys with fear. It was apparent that he had never met her before, probably hadn't even heard of her, so I wasn't quite sure why he was so afraid. Was it just because she was Hades' daughter that she was so feared? Or was it something more?

"That's not possible. Hades can't conceive a child, it would mean—" Prometheus began. I didn't know what it would mean and was hoping he would go on. Apparently there was something more to all this. As to what that was, I wasn't sure.

Chrys didn't say anything, but kept close to me. A.J. was the one who stepped forward. "It's true. She is the daughter of Hades and Persephone. We came up here with the use of Persephone's rings."

Prometheus shook his head. "No, no, no. You need to go back before he sees you, before he comes and destroys all of us here."

"Who comes?" I asked.

"Zeus. Now hurry, I will help you get to where you need to go. I presume you came by boat?"

All three of us nodded.

"Fine, then we should go there right away. Otherwise this could be the start of another great war."

Chapter 17

Chrys

I wasn't supposed to let anyone know I was on Earth, but now at least three gods knew. This wasn't good. If any of them talked to my mother, I would be in deep trouble. I just wanted to go home, praying that Father would never find out.

This had been a mistake, and by the face Prometheus made, I knew that to be a fact. He looked shocked and afraid of what Zeus could do. I knew Prometheus's story, all the gods did. He was a titan who sided with Zeus during the war against

Cronus but got on Zeus' bad side when he stole fire from the gods and gave it to the humans. As punishment, he nailed Prometheus to a cave, letting an eagle tear his insides out until Hercules came thousands of years later and killed the bird. Then, thousands of years after that, Zeus released him.

So yeah, he had a reason to be afraid of Zeus.

I couldn't imagine what he would do when he found out Father had been hiding me all these years. On top of what he had done to Prometheus, I heard of other stories involving his wrath. There was the war with the giants, when Zeus practically fought them all; his battle with Typhon as he tried to defeat Zeus and take over Olympus; then there was Salmoneus and his brothers who imitated Zeus and were killed for that. So many stories involved with Zeus killing someone. Or sleeping with someone. Either one, really.

Not to mention he made my father stay in the Underworld all this time. Even though my father was the oldest, he still got the short end of the stick. Then there was Melinoe. I couldn't believe that my mother had another child, and I was just now hearing about it. Did Father know, or was this one her little secret? He probably did know and just didn't want me to find out about it. Things got complicated when gods fraternized with one another. That was also why Father didn't want me to leave the palace. There was just so much drama.

I still didn't quite understand why it was much of a problem for me to exist. All the other gods had children, yet for some reason it was wrong for me to be alive. Father always said it had to do with the power I possess, but I wanted to hear it from someone on the outside, someone who wasn't my father.

"Prometheus," I began as we walked down the empty streets of London. "Why is it such a big problem that I exist? Why are you so afraid that Zeus will find me?"

He sighed, as if just thinking about Zeus exhausted him. "It's got to do with a lot more than just you. As I said, your father shouldn't have been able to have you, he is the God of Death and having a child is the opposite of death. Your mother is the daughter of Demeter, the Goddess of Harvest and Fertility, yes, but it should never have been possible."

"But why would Zeus care? Why would he want to punish me for being alive?"

He stopped and turned to me. "What is your power? Hmm? The combination of those two, I can only imagine?"

I shook my head. "I don't know what you mean."

"I mean, what can you do as a goddess?"

"I… I can make things move. When my emotions are out of control, I sort of black out. And Father is teaching me how to judge the dead, is that what you mean?"

Prometheus sighed. "Great, your powers have been suppressed. At least he won't be able to detect you due to your power output. Then again, they could arise if provoked." He shot a look at Pothos.

Pothos held up his hands. "Hey, I didn't realize she wasn't supposed to be here. I thought she was like Melinoe or something."

"Yeah, sure."

Melinoe placed her arm around Prometheus. "Prometheus knows that there is only one of me, don't you darling?"

He nodded, a little reluctantly, might I add. "Yeah, there aren't that many out there like you…"

"Thank Zeus," Pothos coughed. Melinoe glared at him, her eyes turning black. Suddenly a black shadow surrounded Pothos. He held up his hand. "Stop! We need to focus on the situation at hand, Melinoe. You can haunt me later."

I thought about the shadows that would appear when I was angry, how everything turns dark. I didn't know exactly what sort of power it was as it felt like raw power, nothing specific. It wasn't like nightmares or love or water or fire. It was just… power.

The shadows disappeared, and Melinoe sighed. "Fine. Whatever."

Huntley put his hand into mine as we kept moving down the streets. I wished my father had explained it to me a bit better, though maybe he had hidden the truth for a reason. He was overprotective, yes, but I was beginning to understand what his brothers were capable of, and he didn't want them to take away the only thing he always wanted. A child. Me.

The boat was actually quite a distance away from where we had first appeared on this plane. It would take a good hour walking before we would reach it. I prayed that nothing would get in our way, not that I could imagine anything really getting in our way. *What were the odds, right?*

Well, apparently the odds were high because the moment we stepped around a corner, there was a man standing there, smiling as if he had hit the jackpot. He had dark wavy hair, dark eyes, a scruffy face.

I didn't know if he was human or god, as I didn't know exactly what each god or goddess looked like and they changed fashion and hair throughout the years, but by the way he was looking at us, and the shock Prometheus had on his face, he had to have been a god.

"Dad," A.J. was the first to speak. "What are you doing here?"

Chapter 18

Huntley

Did he just say dad?

We were up shit creek. If this was A.J.'s dad, that meant he was Poseidon, and Hades and Zeus' bro. He didn't hold a trident like he did in all the school history books I had destroyed over the years, but he did have quite the chiseled face that made me understand why A.J. was so good looking. Damn all these gods and goddesses for appearing so perfect in contrast to us mere mortals.

Poseidon stood there, examining us. No one

moved, as if it would make a difference. Deer in the headlights instinct, I swore. He had caught us and since he was one of the big three, he probably would tell his brother Zeus about us.

But then again, he still didn't know about Chrys yet. She could simply be someone he didn't know— just a human or demigoddess. We knew there were a lot of those around, after all. I prayed that would be the case. Then again, his dead son was also standing here and he would probably want to know how that was possible.

"Agenor. How are you on Earth? How did you escape the Underworld?" he asked as he glanced at the rest of us. "And find yourself in the company of a *titan*?"

Damn, these gods really didn't like titans, did they?

"Excuse me, I helped defeat Cronus, didn't I? Stop regarding me as something inferior to you Olympian gods. I was once more powerful than you could ever imagine," Prometheus commented. It sounded as if he had to justify himself quite often. I could relate, as I was the only human here.

"How long exactly did Zeus have you hanging off that rock? A long time right? If you were so mighty, maybe you should have released yourself."

Oh, burn. The gods liked to hit someone while they were down. I guess when you had nothing else to do for centuries, you got better at your comebacks.

Prometheus didn't say a word. I wasn't quite sure what that was all about. I would ask Chrys after we got out of this safely. That was if we got out of this. I had never felt my heart beating so fast until this moment, not even when we couldn't find Chrys earlier. I wouldn't be surprised if I died of a heart attack.

"So, back to my question." Poseidon turned to his son. "How are you here?"

A.J. was silent for a moment, as if debating telling the truth. I didn't know what the consequences would be for lying to a god, nor did I know what I would do in his place.

Lie. Yup, that's what I would do. That's what I always do.

"I stole one of Persephone's rings and made my great escape," A.J. finally said. It was definitely not believable, and I would need to teach him how to lie later.

He raised an eyebrow. "Really? That's interesting." He stood there for a moment, thinking about this information. I knew that not many ever came back to Earth after, well, dying, so I could understand his surprise. "Then what about these two?"

Poseidon was looking at us. *Shit.*

"Others in the Underworld that wanted to escape. That's all."

He was quiet for a moment. "That would mean you had stayed in the palace and were never sent to one of the three afterlives."

"That's right," A.J. said. "We all became servants to Hades. We couldn't stand it any longer, so we made an escape with Persephone's rings. You know how she is: sneaking people in and out of the Underworld. She's a first rate whore."

Poseidon laughed. "Isn't that a fact. And I think

Melinoe can agree."

She didn't say anything but simply glared at Poseidon. It was apparent that she didn't like him either, which made me even more concerned. She appeared as strong as Chrys, and if she feared Poseidon, then we probably stood no chance.

I kept Chrys close, grabbing her hand and squeezing it tight. I didn't want anything to happen to her and I would stop at nothing to keep her safe. Then again, she probably had a better chance against this guy than I did. But I still wanted to be there for her.

"However, I find it hard to believe that this girl here." His attention turned straight to Chrys. "Is a human or demigod. Her scent." He took a deep breath and let it out slowly. "Is too much like Persephone's."

He stepped up closer to her, but I kept myself between him and Chrys. He raised his eyebrow. "You, however, are just a mere human. Do you really think standing in my way would make any difference?"

"I won't let you come near her, if that's what you mean."

He swatted me away like a pesky fly. There wasn't even any effort put in it, just a flick of the wrist and I went crashing into the brick building next to me.

And I thought my shoulder hurt before all this happened.

"Huntley!" Chrys cried out. She looked as if she was going to run after me, but Poseidon grabbed her jaw.

"Let me look at you," he said as he peered into her eyes. Like she had a choice with his hand clenching her jaw. It was kind of disgusting how he was looking at her, especially since he was her uncle, right? Chrys told me never to think about family relationships in the mortal sense within the family of the gods. That it would just make my head spin. I now understood what she meant by that. "You may look and smell like your mother but you definitely have your daddy's eyes, don't you, daughter of Hades?"

I could see the shock on Chrys' face. She didn't think it would be that obvious to people out of the Underworld. Hell, I didn't think with all the people in the world, with all the gods that there were, that anyone could tell just by looking at her. Apparently we were wrong.

This was a big mistake.

I didn't know what to do. If Hades was here, I knew he could stop this, he could save his daughter. But he wasn't here, nor did he know we were on Earth, so we were all by ourselves, facing gods who have existed for millennia. We were nothing compared to them. I was just a human. Why did I think I could protect her? Why did I think I could make a difference?

Slowly standing up, I knew that even if I was a human, that I probably could be easily squashed by anyone here, but I wouldn't give up. I would do everything I could to protect Chrys.

"Let her go!" I demanded.

He ignored me, acted as if I wasn't even there. Typical. "Where's your daddy, daughter of Hades?

He should be protecting such a priceless gem—"

"Father, let her go," A.J. spoke up. It was about time. Here I was busting my ass and he just watched as his father was hurting our friend, the one we swore we would protect on Earth.

Poseidon turned to A.J. but didn't let go of Chrys' jaw. I could see her cringe from how hard he was squeezing her. "What? Is this your mistress? Is this why you were serving in Hades' palace, because you fell in love with his daughter?"

A.J. didn't say anything, but the eye contact between Chrys and him spoke more than any words, especially since they weren't denying it. Apparently, something had gone on between them before I came around. I felt a little shock go through my heart at this realization. I really thought they were just friends this entire time, but apparently there had been something going on between them, whether it was still going on was something I didn't even want to ponder at this moment in time.

Poseidon smiled. "So I was right, you like her. *Pathetic.*"

Prometheus spoke up. "Probably just likes sleeping around like his father. Everyone thinks Zeus has had a lot of chicks, but really you are the slut of the family, aren't you?"

I wasn't sure why Prometheus was brave enough to make comments like that to Poseidon, yet terrified of Zeus. I guess after dealing with the gods so much, he just didn't care anymore, Zeus being the only exception. That, or he was trying to distract him from Chrys. Melinoe was still silent, not sure as to what to say to him.

"Let her go, Father, none of this is your concern!"

He raised an eyebrow. "It isn't? You're in my domain, are you not? The moment you stepped on Earth, I had control over you. You should know this, Agenor. Besides…" He turned to Chrys again. "I don't think I can say no to this quest."

He pulled Chrys in and stole a kiss from her. At first she was surprised and then disgusted, trying to push him away but finding that he was stronger.

I was just about to run to her, as if I could do anything about it, as was A.J. when we felt it in the air. the wind was beginning to pick up, the air becoming colder and darkening. I glanced over to Melinoe, hoping that maybe it was her. By the look on her face, along with Pothos and Prometheus, I could tell it was none of them.

It was Chrys, and with her anger, her power level was rising. She was going to destroy everything around her once her fury was unleashed.

Chapter 19

Chrys

I could feel the power surge through my veins. I didn't care anymore, if this god knew who I was, then word would go out to Zeus about me. Hiding this seemed impossible now, and since Poseidon was threatening me, I wasn't going to hold back any longer.

The darkness that always consumed me came pouring out. I loved the feeling it gave me, the feeling that I was in charge. At last I could unleash it all, all the frustration my fate has put on me. Finally,

I had a reason to.

With a quick motion of my hand, I pushed him back into the wall. He went crashing into the side of the building, bricks shattering on impact. There was no backing away now.

"Get away from me!" I ordered. I had so much energy raging through my body that I couldn't hold back at this point. Darkness and light felt like it was swirling through my mind. I knew I had the power to destroy everything around me. I had been suppressing it because of Father's orders, but he wasn't here. Now I had to show the gods what I was really made of.

Apparently A.J. and Huntley had other ideas.

Huntley hurried to my side. "Chrys, please calm down. You need to stay calm."

I shook my head. "No. It's too late. I'm not backing down on this one. If I'm going down, it won't be without a fight."

"Chrys, think this through," A.J. added. "We need to run away right now to the boat. We need to get out of here and back to the Underworld before it's too late."

"No!" I lashed out, clenching handfuls of my hair. "I'm not going to keep hiding. I can't do it anymore! There's no point, Poseidon will tell Zeus. My secret is out in the open now. "

Prometheus came over and put his hands on my shoulders. "You need to get out of here. You don't understand the severity of Zeus' wrath. With a snap of his fingers, he can throw you into Tartarus. You won't even see your father before that moment, he won't even have a say. Do you want to put your father through that? When he spent all this time trying to protect you?"

I stared into Prometheus's blue eyes. He was right, I needed to get out of here. There was no way I could completely defeat Poseidon, even with the power emanating from me like this. I tried to take deep breaths, but it wasn't working. There was too much power.

"I can't. I can't stop shaking."

Prometheus wrapped his arms around me. "Shhh. It's alright. Deep breaths, we are all in this together, okay? Pothos, Melinoe, and I will make sure you get back home in one piece."

I heard laughter from behind him. We all turned to find Poseidon standing up, a cocky grin on his face. "Oh yeah? You and what army?"

He held out his hand, water coming from all around formed into a trident. I had never seen anything like it. It was like something out of a movie, pretty cool if I wasn't going to be stabbed with it at any given moment.

But Prometheus was right, we should have ran.

"Daughter of Hades, I give you one last warning. Come with me and you and your friends won't be harmed. Resist and I will have to destroy them one by one." Droplets of water coming from the water that accumulated around were now forming into swirls around him. He was getting ready to attack.

Pothos, Prometheus, and Melinoe all stepped up in front of me.

"Go, we will hold him off. Get to the boat and get out of here," Prometheus exclaimed. "Go now!"

Huntley grabbed my hand, and with A.J. running

close behind, we ran towards where we had left the boat.

I couldn't believe that the three of them would stand up to Poseidon like that, in order to protect me. They didn't know me, yet they were quick to fight for me. I didn't understand why they would do such a thing. They had to have had other reasons to want to fight him, to not fear what he was capable of.

I didn't look back. I knew that if I did, the power would surge through me once again and I couldn't let that happen. I would lose control and I didn't know what would happen if that were the case. London was too pretty to almost destroy in a fit of rage. I just prayed we would reach the boat before Poseidon caught up with us.

We ran as hard as we could. Although I knew my legs wouldn't wear out as easily as humans, I could tell that Huntley was struggling to keep up. He was the only human out of all of us, I didn't even think about that. He stood no chance if we had to battle Poseidon on our own. He was always trying to protect me this whole time, it was time that I would make sure he was protected.

No one seemed to care that we were running past, clearly trying to escape danger. Huntley had said earlier that cities were strange like that, people ignoring everything around them so easily. I would think they would want to care more, but I guess not. That was the way of the world.

I still felt the energy surge in my chest, but I didn't let it become unleashed. If I did that, I would surely hurt Huntley as he had his hand in mine. I couldn't let that happen, I wouldn't hurt him with my own hands.

I was surprised that A.J. had gone up against his father like he had just moments before. I knew they didn't have much contact when he was growing up, but that didn't mean he wasn't still family. I was also surprised that he didn't deny Poseidon's accusations about loving me. I knew he didn't, but why he would outright lie, I wasn't sure. He could have just been hoping that Poseidon would simply go away. It didn't work, though, it just made

Poseidon want to capture me even more.

Huntley, however, thought A.J.'s silence meant that he did in fact like me. I knew it probably frustrated him, made him wonder what all had gone on in the millennia that we had been friends. But I knew clearing it up later would be much easier than trying to explain it now.

A loud crash sounded in front of us. We all stopped to find Pothos on the ground. He had been thrown from where they had been fighting all the way to where we were standing. He looked hurt, bleeding out onto the pavement. He was still conscious though, as he tried to pull himself up, stumbling from the pain.

We finally turned around to find Poseidon standing there. What he had done to Prometheus and Melinoe, I wasn't sure.

"Last chance, daughter of Hades. It's your call."

Before I could say anything, both A.J. and Huntley stood in front of me, guarding me with their lives. I wanted to tell them to stop, that this was my battle, but it was no use. They had their minds made up.

That, and with a flick of a hand, Poseidon made a wall of water rise before him and let it knock them straight into the building beside us.

"Huntley! A.J.!" I exclaimed. Both were lying on the ground now in defeat, soaked from Poseidon's attack.

"Ah, so you care more about that human than my son. That clears that up then."

I glared at him, shaking my head. "I won't go down without a fight. And when my father hears about this, he—"

"He will what? Your father isn't here." He gestured around. "He isn't coming to your rescue, not in my domain. He knows better than that. It was you who was at fault—you who left his little cozy home. His safe haven. Have you ever heard of your father leaving his realm before? Helping out anywhere other than his own domain? No, he won't leave that place. He knows his daughter made her mistake and must pay the price."

I did want to listen to what he was saying, but to believe that he would come to my rescue. He always did, but this time I knew I was on my own. I had lied to him, he probably didn't even know I was here. I had dug my own grave this time.

I clenched my fist. No, I didn't care if this was a god of Olympus, Poseidon himself. I could win at a fight against him. I *would* win a fight against him. I just had to tap into the strength, building up from inside my core, and find a way to control it just enough to use it to its full extent against Poseidon. It was the only way to win.

"Then I guess the only person who can save me is myself."

I broke the seal, the seal my father had told me to keep tight all these years, the one that stored all the power that at times seeped out. Huntley didn't even know that the power he had witnessed over these past couple of years was just the tip of the iceberg. These gods knew I existed now. There was no reason to hide it.

Black shadows and blinding light came pouring out of my fingertips, destroying everything it touched. Poseidon motioned his hands and a wave of water came crashing down towards me. I flicked my hand and the light and shadow pushed it back, making the water fall to the ground. Simple. I doubted he would be any match if he kept that up.

I shouldn't act so cocky. It didn't fit me as I had been stupid and didn't notice that Poseidon was stepping closer. When the surrounding water vanished, he grabbed my wrist. He was much stronger than I when it came to physical strength. I tried to pull my arms back, but he wouldn't budge.

"You don't scare me. You are but a weakling to me." He forced a kiss on me. My anger rose, as did my power. He moved his head back. "And you made a big mistake. We are near water, my power source."

And without a second thought, he jumped into the River Thames, pulling me along with him.

Chapter 20

Huntley

"Chrys!" I yelled out as I watched Poseidon pull her into the water. I got up, my body aching, screaming at me to not move, especially my shoulder, but I had to see if she was alright. I had to see if she somehow got out of his grip and had swam back up to the surface.

There was nothing, not even a movement in the water.

Did she even know how to swim? I mean, I didn't think the palace had a pool or anything in it, not to mention these waters looked pretty disgusting. It was hard enough when you could see where you were swimming to. A river like that was probably nearly impossible to swim in if one hadn't had proper training.

I smacked my hand on the railing in frustration over the situation. What do I do now? It wasn't like I could go after her. It was pitch black, and he was a god. He could easily be long gone by now to wherever he was taking her. Would it be like *The Little Mermaid*'s palace or something? Fuck, I didn't know anymore. I didn't know what to do, how we were going to get out of this one.

A.J. hurried to my side. He appeared as hurt as I did, scrapes covering his body. I couldn't believe he would go up against Poseidon, his own father, like he did. I was really surprised.

"What do we do now?" I whispered. "How do we get her back?"

A.J. shook his head. "I don't know…"

"What happened?" A voice behind us asked.

I turned around to find Prometheus hurrying to

us, along with Melinoe. They appeared to be fine, other than their clothes torn to shreds. I had a feeling their skin appeared the same, but they had healed by the time they had reached us. *Lucky them.*

Pothos was still in bad shape as he limped over to us. His wounds were healing slowly but I could see the change coming over him, the battle wounds quickly become fainter scars.

He probably had been injured the most, as he had been thrown a few blocks in distance. Although I still thought he was a creep, and that actually was the reason we were in this mess, I couldn't just forget the fact that he had stood up for Chrys and us. He did care for her safety in the long run, which was strange since they had just met. They must have really been rooting for Hades, I guess.

Looking back down at the water, I answered. "Poseidon grabbed her and dragged her into the water. I don't know what we should do next."

Prometheus shook his head. "None of us here have a chance against him in water, or even could follow him."

I looked back out in the water. There still was no movement. She had to be okay, I couldn't imagine what would happen if she wasn't.

"Then what do we do?" I asked again.

He shrugged. "I really don't know…"

I let out a brief sigh. My mind was at a loss. Especially since I didn't know why most of them were helping us. Sure, Melinoe and Chrys had the same mom, but Prometheus didn't seem to have a reason, especially with his fear of Zeus. Wouldn't he rather turn her in and be on his good side? "Why did you guys help us? It's not like you have any reason to."

Pothos shrugged. "I just hate these gods. And don't want to piss off Hades. He's the nicest one out there. He gets a bad rap, especially because of the rumors Poseidon, Zeus, and Demeter start about him, and Persephone will never stand up for him. She knows she is the only one who can correct the rumors since rarely anyone else sees him. Honestly, I think the three of them are the reason she acts the way she does. She used to love Hades but then she hung out with those three and other gods and she became... different."

Melinoe nodded. "I agree, Hades is a great guy. And Chrys' kind of sister and we sisters need to stand up for each other."

Wait, were there others?

Prometheus scratched the scruff on his chin. "I know the things that Zeus and Poseidon do, the things they get away with. Hades is never given a break, no other god other than the two of them are ever given a break. I wanted to get her out of here before either of them found her. More importantly Zeus. For once I wanted to see Hades get his way, but nevertheless his siblings stand in his way. But this time I doubt Hades will go down without a fight. This is going to turn into a war, you can count on that."

I closed my eyes. This was all my fault. I should have talked her out of it. I shouldn't have let her come. Now Prometheus was talking about a war, for crying out loud. Could this get any more complicated?

Suddenly water started thrashing about. Something was happening underneath the water. I didn't know whether to lean against the railing to get a better look, or stay away from the water before whatever it was showed itself. Being the dumb human I was, I leaned against the railing.

Out of nowhere, a large object came shooting out of the water and rammed straight into Tower Bridge. Whatever it was, stayed there, pinned to the brick.

Then I realized what it was. It was Poseidon.

Shit, I couldn't decide if this was good or bad. I mean, if someone saw... I don't know, what would they do? Call the cops? And tell them what, a goddess was going berserk? Yeah, I bet they would come running for that one. Take your meds and go back to bed, Fred.

Chrys ascended out of the water as if she was a demon coming out of hell, which frankly she kind of was. And she definitely looked like it at this point. Her eyes were jet black, shadows and light swirling all around her. She didn't look like herself, she appeared like a monster ready to destroy everything that sought to oppose her.

I had seen her angry plenty of times, but this was a completely different kind of anger. First off, she had every right to be pissed, but this wasn't normal human anger. This was an angry goddess type of fury, a goddess that could bring death on anything she touched. She was the daughter of Hades, it made sense.

And it made me wonder what her father was truly capable of. I shuddered at the thought.

"This isn't good," Prometheus whispered.

I looked at him. He was worried, watching as Chrys flew over to where she had pinned Poseidon. "What do you mean? She has used her powers before. Not this much but—"

"She's in the sky. It's only a matter of time…" He rubbed his temples. "I've got to get out of here."

Prometheus turned and ran off. I thought about calling after him, but knew it was useless. He was too keen on running away at this point, afraid of something. Weren't we all afraid at this point? His sudden departure made me worry even more. Chrys had the upper hand now. What could go wrong? After she knocks him out, we can make a run for it.

Pothos and Melinoe stayed with A.J. and I, though, watching what Chrys was about to do to Poseidon as he had been pinned to the Tower Bridge. His arms were stretched out, as if he were a martyr. I prayed that he didn't escape, otherwise he would destroy the entire city. Or at least, I figured he could destroy the whole entire city of London effortlessly. I knew Chrys could…

Chrys put her hand forward, shadows and light shooting straight at Poseidon. It hit him straight in the chest. He screamed out in pain.

"Not good, not good, not good," Melinoe mumbled.

"What? She's teaching him not to mess with her. He deserves it."

She shook her head. "No, what she is shooting him with. It's more powerful than anything I have ever seen. It is darkness, and life combined. She is literally bringing death upon Poseidon, then life again. He is dying over and over again, which is a lot of power to have, even for a god. It's hard enough to kill one of us, let alone do it over and over again and bring them back to life. She controls too much power. That is why Hades has kept her hidden..."

I tried to understand what she was trying to say, but I barely understood what went on with the gods. I was lost. Too much was going on right now to deal with any of it. I just wanted to get out of this place and go back to the Underworld.

That's when it happened. Thunder roared in the sky. Before my mind could even register what was going on, lightning came shooting out of the sky and straight at Chrys, followed by another loud crackle of thunder. She was thrown back towards us, hitting the ground just behind me, skidding for at least a hundred feet.

I didn't even have time to go to her side before something stepped out of the sky and onto the pavement in front of us. It was a man with blond hair, blue eyes, and an air about him that meant business.

He looked down at Chrys. "Well, well. What do we have here?"

Chapter 21

Chrys

I gasped for air as every nerve in my body cried out in agony. *What the fuck was that?* I felt like I was hit by lightning, and if I wasn't mistaken, that was what I had seen. I never realized how painful it would be to have such a shock knock me back. Whatever it was, it was going to pay. Big time. I was sick and tired of all the shit that had been going on lately. There was no more holding back. I would get my revenge.

Speaking of which, what had I been doing before

all this happened? Everything was still a blur, but I remembered Poseidon taking me down into the water.

Death and life. That was what my power truly was. I could create and destroy everything. I knew my power was dark; I knew I could destroy so much around me, but I never realized that I could bring it back—that I could summon life just like my mother.

Then it hit me. I was summoning life and death upon Poseidon, killing him over and over again. Father had warned me about using those powers, that it was against nature, against the laws that held the universe together. If anyone found out about it, I would be in deep shit.

But I guess it was too late for that now. I had used my powers out in the open for all of London to see. Not to mention I used my powers on my uncle, Poseidon, one of the big three. There was no way this could be a secret any longer.

I opened my eyes to find a blond man standing over me. He needed a haircut and to shave, as he looked a bit shaggy, but I guess that was the style now. I preferred my father's clean-shaven look for older men. Speaking of which, he kind of looked like my father, if my father had blond hair...

My heart practically stopped as I looked up at this man. He still appeared smug as he seemed to be waiting for me to respond. It couldn't be, could it? My eyes slowly went towards the light that was coming from his hand. It looked like a lightning bolt. It *was* a lightning bolt.

Shit. Shit, shit, shit, shit... Shit.

I rose to my feet as quickly as I could, backing away from the man before me. Backing away from Zeus himself.

He stepped one stride towards me, still intrigued. "I saw your little show, young lass. So please, tell me, who exactly are you?"

I couldn't speak, couldn't do anything but stand there like an idiot, because I really was an idiot. My most dreaded nightmare faced me, the one person who I was supposed to stay away from, the person who would determine my fate if he ever found out I existed. I had completely failed my father. And for that, I was going to die, I just knew it. It wasn't fair, none of it was fair. I just wanted to be free, I didn't want this god-crap any more. But that would never happen. I should have just listened to my father. I should have just stayed hidden.

"You're…. You're…" I mumbled.

"Zeus, the God of Olympus, God of Order and Nature, yes. I am the god all the other gods take orders from, the one who makes sure everything is working how it should, that life and death follow the rules I had put into place—The rules of nature." He glanced over to where Poseidon hung on the bridge.

Wow, did I do that? I guess I did, though, in my defense, he did try to drag me down to his ocean palace, and I didn't even want to think about what would have happened then. Yeah, he pretty much deserved everything I had thrown at him.

Zeus went on, "seems you have slipped from my sight, because I would have never let any god have as much power as you seem to have."

I could feel my heart pounding in my chest. I couldn't move, couldn't do anything against this god. And, as he said, he was the God of Gods, he could do whatever he wanted with me, he had the power. I could never stand up against him. I was royally screwed.

"So answer me, who are you?" he asked once more. Even though he appeared he was being patient with me, I could tell that patience was wearing thin.

I took a deep breath, trying to calm myself down. There was no point in lying now. When Poseidon woke up (at least I think he could wake up after everything I did to him), Zeus would learn the truth. I had wasted all the work my father had put into keeping this secret. It was time to come clean and pay the price of what I had done. So I did the only thing I could do—stand tall and accept my fate. "I am Chrysanthemum, daughter of Hades and Persephone."

Zeus raised an eyebrow. "Daughter of *Hades*? That's impossible. He can't bear any children. He is the God of Death, I made sure conceiving children would be impossible for him."

I shrugged. "Well, I guess you messed up." Stupid thing to say to the God of Gods, but let's be honest, he did mess up. If he supposedly made it so my father couldn't have children, then I was living proof of that mistake.

Zeus circled me, examining every inch of my body, a little creepily might I add. I knew I looked like a wreck at this point. My dress was soaked, there was algae covering my tights, my hair was a tangled mess. I didn't even want to know what my makeup looked like at this point. Not that it mattered, it wasn't like I wanted to look good for this ass or anything. He was going to kill me, anyway.

"You definitely have your mother's body, and her scent." He stopped in front of me, staring into my eyes. "But those eyes, you have the eyes of death. You have your father's eyes. You are indeed their daughter."

I didn't know what to say to that, other than,

yeah, it's true. Pothos and Poseidon pretty much had said the same thing when they saw me, so there was no denying I looked like my father and mother. The cat was let out of the bag, so to speak. It wasn't like I could have lied straight to Zeus' face. It wouldn't have been that hard for him to figure out who I was, given the power I had.

I still thought it was odd he appeared like he did, as the worlds were vast and he couldn't see everything that was happening all at once. I had been releasing a lot of power though, I was probably like a big beacon. But if that was the case, wouldn't all the gods be here?

Or was I such a monster that they wanted to stay far away?

Zeus examined me for a few more moments, then turned to the others. "Agenor, you spoke the truth. I will hear your plea."

My mouth dropped a little. What did he mean that A.J. had spoken the truth? He couldn't have alerted Zeus about all of this, could he have? That would have been impossible, not to mention A.J.

would never betray me like that. We have been friends for centuries. What would he have gained by telling Zeus? And he had tried to help me against his father when he attacked. It made no sense.

"A.J., what's going on?" I asked.

Zeus laughed. "What does it look like? He alerted me the moment you stepped onto Earth, that you were Hades' daughter. And in return, I was to hear his request."

I couldn't believe what I was hearing, that he would do this to me. Then everything he had said the past few days hit me, why he was so eager to leave the Underworld, why he wanted us on Earth, why he never went to Elysium. He wanted to come back to Earth, to escape the Underworld. After all these years, he held on to that want of freedom. He even said that days before. I had been such a fool.

Before I could say something, before I could tell him what he could do to himself and it would have not been kind, Huntley punched him. Hard. Harder than I had ever seen him punch anything. I mean, if I didn't know him, I would have thought he was a demigod or something, that arm. A.J. hit the ground with a thud.

Pothos and Melinoe held Huntley back before he could lay any more punches on him. Why they stopped him, I wasn't really that sure. A.J. had it coming. Then again, Zeus was right there and probably would have no problem destroying Huntley. If I wasn't so shocked and afraid of Zeus, I would also be sending A.J. to the depths of the Underworld right then and there.

"Traitor!" Huntley yelled at him. "How could you do that to her? She was your friend! You don't betray friends like that!"

A.J. rubbed the blood that had been dripping down his chin. Huntley had hit him good. "Stupid human, you have no idea what's going on do you? What happened when we came to Earth?"

Huntley shook his head. I felt as if my stomach was in my throat. I didn't think they noticed, I didn't think they realized... I wasn't even sure what had happened was real...

A.J. pointed at me. "When she brought us up here,

she made us mortal again! We are alive! We don't have to go back to the Underworld, we can be free! She broke her father's laws, yes, but in doing that we can have our lives back. The Earth is our home, not that dreadful place." He turned to Zeus. "And that is what I want, I want to be immortal and never age. I don't want to go back to the Underworld ever again. I want my life back. I'm a demigod, I do not deserve death. Only humans do."

Zeus appeared as if he was genuinely thinking about granting his request. I mean, could he do that? I had heard stories, but I felt as if this would go against his law of nature and what not. It didn't make sense.

"You may have your life back, but I cannot make you immortal if you have ever eaten or drank anything in the Underworld. By doing so, you tie yourself to the place and must return someday. It's the rule."

A.J. shook his head with a bit of a smirk. "That I know, which is why I have neither taken a bite of food or a sip of drink in that dreadful place."

My eyes widened. How was that possible? After thousands of years, he would have been starving, thirsty beyond belief. No, he couldn't die from not eating or drinking, but he would have been in grave pain the entire time. Even the dead have to consume food and drinks for their bodies. Just the thought of it made my body cringe. If I didn't eat for a few hours, I was cranky, let alone not eating for thousands of years. And there was always food and drink in front of him. How would he have had the strength to resist for such a long time? How would he have the strength to do anything, as a matter of fact? I guess he was a demigod, but still. I was a goddess and I couldn't even imagine.

It was nearly impossible but the more I thought about it, the more I realized every time I ate with him, every time we kicked back and had drinks, he either said he was full or not that thirsty. I couldn't recall one instance that he joined us in eating or drinking.

Zeus looked as shocked as I did. Apparently I wasn't the only one who felt as if this would be impossible, even for a god. "You didn't?"

"No."

Carefully Zeus went on. "You will never grow old and you will never die. But realize that while this may sound like a gift, it can also be a curse. Are you really sure it's something you want?"

A.J. nodded. "I've been thinking about it for thousands of years. I am sure."

"Then your request is granted," Zeus turned back to me. "A request I only had to grant because of the laws you have broken."

Seriously, he blamed me for this? It wasn't like I could have possibly known that was A.J.'s plan all along. I mean, he had to be starving, but it did explain why he ate so much at the restaurant when we first arrived to London. As for why he didn't try to sneak out of the Underworld earlier, well, he must have wanted immortality. And the only way he could have done that is by selling me to Zeus.

Which meant he had been planning all of this since the moment he met me.

I quickly shook my head. "I didn't mean to, I

didn't know—"

"That is irrelevant." The lightning bolt in his hand grew brighter and brighter. He was ready to end it right then and there. He wasn't even going to hear my side of the story. What a dick, seriously. Arrogant as could be.

"I cannot allow such a goddess to exist. Goodbye, Chrysanthemum, daughter of Hades. You will be no more."

He raised the lightning bolt up, the power surging through the air. I knew there was nothing I could do, that my power would never be able to save me. I didn't even have a chance to try to gather my strength as I did with Poseidon. This was the end and everything I wanted to do, wanted to say, would be no more. I just wished I could apologize to my father for being such a stupid daughter.

I closed my eyes and waited for the pain to come and for all of it to be no more.

Chapter 22

Huntley

"No!" I screamed out, Pothos and Melinoe still holding me back. I knew I couldn't do anything, that I would simply perish alongside Chrys the moment the lightning bolt left Zeus' hand. But was living worth it if Chrys wasn't there? I'd rather perish, to be destroyed completely, than face any type of life without her. Even if that meant suffering Tartarus alongside her. I owed her that much.

A.J. simply watched as the girl I thought he cared about, that I thought he would protect with his life just as I would have, was going to be destroyed by Zeus.

Lightning shot forward at Chrys, while light blinded me temporarily. That was it, I thought. Everything was over. Life seemed colorless now, the world devoid of meaning. I never knew love could be so powerful. It had been absent in my life for so long that it was hard for me to even recognize it until now. I loved Chrys and I could never feel any different about her than that.

I didn't know what exactly had happened but when I was able to focus again, there stood Hades between Zeus and his daughter, dressed in black, just as normal, his hand blocking the strike. The light dimmed in his hand and he closed it as if it was nothing, just a little static shock. See, he would make a great movie villain.

"Brother, what a surprise," Zeus commented with a bit of a smile. "I didn't think you would actually come."

"Father," Chrys whispered as she stepped forward toward him. He looked back at her. I couldn't see his face, but from the contrite look Chrys had after they made eye contact, I could tell it had to be one of anger and disappointment. She stopped reaching out to her father and stepped back. Ouch. Knowing Chrys, she probably, unlike me, had never disappointed her father before. And this wasn't like, oh sorry for getting an "F" on my last test, I will do better next time. This was a matter of life and death for both of them. This mistake could lead to an all-out war between Zeus and Hades. I wished I could help her, but there was nothing I could do.

A.J. bolted. And I mean *bolted*. He was long gone, ran away faster than Prometheus had. He knew the moment Hades found out what he had done, he would have dragged him down to Tartarus himself. It didn't matter what magic Zeus had placed on him. Hades watched as he ran off, probably figuring he had something to do with all of this. But at the same time, he knew that if he moved, Zeus would hurt his daughter. He would deal with A.J. later, and hopefully I would have front row seats to that showdown.

Hades turned back to Zeus. "What do you think you are doing?"

"You know perfectly well what I have to do. She can't exist, not if we want to keep order in the universe. Her power is too great, no god should be able to have authority over life and death like that. We have already discussed this. You weren't supposed to have any children. It's against everything we stand for."

"I can train her, I can make sure she doesn't use her powers against the laws. Just don't kill my daughter. She doesn't deserve any of this."

Zeus shook his head and pointed at Poseidon. "Look at our brother, Hades! Do you see what she is capable of? She killed him and brought him back to life again and again. You may be able to train her, but if she loses control even more, she could destroy this world and everything in it! She can destroy all of us when she is old enough, just like the prophet said! Can't you see that?"

Whoa. A prophet? What did he mean by that?

Was there some kind of prophecy that said Chrys was going to bring about Ragnarok or something?

Hades shook his head. "I don't care, she is still my baby girl and I will protect her no matter the cost."

Zeus let out a brief laugh. "You think you are so mighty brother, but you know you are not the one in charge. You are stuck in your own little world, without the company of other gods. You forget that this world and Olympus doesn't revolve around you, that you aren't even supposed to be here. You have no say or jurisdiction anywhere other than in your home."

Wow, and I thought my family liked to put me down. Here, the God of Death was being told he was worthless and didn't matter anywhere except in hiding. Geez, I wouldn't ever want to go to that family's Thanksgiving dinner.

"You hide me away in the Underworld only because you fear me and what I can do. I am much more powerful than you and Poseidon, and you are afraid my daughter is the same. It isn't about keeping order you are worried about, but protecting your own skin."

"Oh really? You think so?"

So, yeah, the gods are fighting. The rest of us were kind of just standing here, waiting for something. We really couldn't do anything, so yeah... Shit was going on all around us and all we could do was watch. I felt so worthless right now.

Then again, there were also gods just standing here as well, so I felt a bit better about myself.

"I do. After the prophecy of Metis' child destroying you, and you destroying that child just like Cronus tried to do to us, there was another prophecy—the prophecy of a child of death bringing change to all the worlds. That was why you forbade me from having children, but you don't even know if it was this child she was talking about. I won't allow you to harm her because of your paranoia. I'm telling you now that I am taking Chrys back with me to the Underworld, a place that you can never reach her. She will forever be in my protection and I can guarantee that she will never set foot on this world again."

"Just like you told her never to come here before? I see that worked so well the first time."

"I doubt she would ever disobey me a second time," Hades growled.

"And you can guarantee that?"

"I can."

Zeus laughed. "You really are stubborn, aren't you, brother? Strict and stubborn."

Yeah, look who's talking…

"It was no wonder that she tried to escape your grasp and ran away. She couldn't stand being around you any longer, much like with Persephone."

"That's not true," Chrys exclaimed. "He's a loving father that has always been there for me!"

Zeus smiled. "Oh how sweet, she's defending you. Then why did you destroy all his hard work of hiding you by coming out into the open like this? How could you betray him like that?"

"I… I didn't think…"

"That's right, you *didn't* think. And now your father has left his position, his busy schedule, to come and save you, not to mention the threat of a war brewing because of your simple mistake."

A war? They couldn't be serious, could they? What did that even entail, when gods went to war? From all the stories, it made it sound like the Earth was always the battleground, the thing that gets hurt the most in a clash between immortals. There hadn't been a war like that for thousands and thousands of years. Humans had developed so much since then. I couldn't imagine what a war of that scale would do to the Earth as it was.

I had to look deep down to see whether I really cared. I did, but it took a while. Although there were a lot of things I hated about this world, there were a lot good things about it too. For instance, tea.

"Please, don't. I'll go back. I won't cause any more trouble. Please, just stop," Chrys pleaded.

"It's too late for that and your father knows it. Now, it's his decision. Hand you over or start a fight between the two of us. Which is it going to be, brother? After all these years?"

Hades stared at him for a moment, contemplating

what to do next, I figured. "Huntley, take Chrys and get back to the Underworld. Chrys, take this." He handed her something, it looked like a helmet. Like a cool Spartan helmet. "Now run."

I grabbed Chrys' hand, and we ran away from where Hades and Zeus stood, intense power radiating off both of them, just waiting for the time for all their pent-up power to erupt all at once. Whatever was about to happen, I didn't want to be around when it exploded. Melinoe and Pothos followed after us, wanting to clear the area as well.

Then it started. A thunderous roar of power echoing throughout the city. The battle had begun.

Chapter 23

Chrys

It sounded like thunder, an explosion of sorts. It was louder than anything I had ever heard, the energy nearly pushing me down on the ground. I knew the power my father had was beyond anything I could ever have imagined, but that still didn't mean he could take on Zeus like he was. I hoped that he would succeed, that we could get to the Underworld safely and things would go back to normal, but I knew that wasn't possible. Zeus was the God of Gods for a reason. If Father could have taken him out, he would have done so long ago. We could never go back to normal, not after the shit I caused.

The way he looked at me, his anger and disappointment in his eyes, I knew I would never get that out of my mind. I had never done anything to hurt my father before, and he had never done anything to deserve the situation I had put him in. I had disobeyed him, causing this vicious battle before me, causing him having to fight his brother. He could lose because of me, and what then?

I'd rather die than let anything happen to my father, especially since it would be my fault. All of this was my fault, putting Huntley in harm's way, bringing my father into this. If only I had figured out A.J.'s intentions. This was all because of him, because he wanted to live forever on Earth.

No, I couldn't place all the blame on him. I knew the risks; he didn't force me. I just had been so mad at my mother that I wanted to know what Earth was like, how she could think it was better than life in the Underworld with me and Father. I still didn't understand, but that was because in the past hour I had been almost kidnapped and almost killed so I couldn't really talk.

I could see why my father didn't want anything to do with his own family, though. It didn't seem like they got along even before this. However, being forced to stay in the Underworld, Father had held much resentment against his brothers during that time, so them threatening me was just the tip of the iceberg needed for him to explode in retaliation.

But that didn't mean I didn't make it worse. I was the catalyst to all of this.

And what was this prophecy about? That the daughter of death would bring change upon all the worlds? Why did no one tell me this? Was I the daughter of darkness? No, I couldn't be. I couldn't change the world, I was just some goddess who should have never left her spoiled little world. There was no way I could take out Zeus, not when my father was having trouble doing that very same task. It had to have been someone else, even my father said that.

But then why didn't he tell me sooner?

Gaia had predicted that the son of Zeus born by Metis would become stronger than Zeus and overpower him. So he killed Metis' unborn child, as apparently deities do to solve their problems. So I could see why even Father didn't think I was part of the prophecy, and wanted me to stay clear of Zeus. I just wished he had told me that whole story earlier. Maybe it would have made a difference. Probably not.

We stopped a little distance away from the battle and I looked down at the helmet in my hand. It was old, worn, like every other relic in the Underworld. It was Father's helmet of invisibility. No one would be able to find us if I used it, and we all joined hands.

"What is that?" Huntley asked. I glanced over at Pothos and Melinoe. I could tell they already knew exactly what it was.

"It's the helmet of invisibility." I held out my hands to the others. "If we all gather hands, we can disappear."

"Well, why didn't you say so earlier?" Huntley grabbed my right hand and Melinoe my left, with Pothos holding her hand. I put the crown on, and we turned invisible.

Under the helmet of invisibility, we hurried as fast as we could towards the boat. This was our only chance, and I knew Father could easily travel to the Underworld after his fight. He didn't even need a boat as he knew where all the secret passages were. I wondered what would happen after we made it through this, if we made it through this, that is. I don't know what Father will do to me now, how harsh his punishment will be, whether he would ever trust me again.

I didn't want to lose his trust. My father was one of the most important people in my life, if not the most important. I looked up to him, loved him with all my heart. Yet I still betrayed him like I did. I had really thought it would all be okay, that he wouldn't find out, that he was just exaggerating the dangers of me leaving the Underworld. Apparently I was wrong.

We kept running. I wasn't quite sure why Pothos and Melinoe were still at our side, why they didn't run off like Prometheus did. Or I guess that's what had happened as he was gone by the time Zeus knocked me out of the sky. He probably knew Zeus was coming and didn't want any part in that fight. I couldn't blame him really. I was surprised he even stuck around for that long.

So for Melinoe and Pathos, maybe they just felt sorry for me or didn't get along with Zeus or Poseidon. Maybe they just wanted an adventure, who knew their reasons. Gods were weird as I was finding out. And humans. And demigods. Everything was just strange. Hopefully, maybe later, I'd learn why they were willing to follow my lead. That is, if I ever saw them again.

After rounding the corner, we came upon a woman. We all stopped, forgetting for a moment that we were invisible. She had long curly brown hair, a long white dress with gold accenting it. I had never seen something look so beautiful and so pure. I gaped at the sight of her. She only could be one person, and that was Athena.

Her eyes were closed as she held a spear and shield, as if meditating. I had heard stories of her heroic deeds and how she was loyal to Zeus. He must have called upon her to help him find me. The four of us quietly started to turn around to sneak away, but it was useless. She could somehow sense us.

"Daughter of Hades! You are to surrender now and be taken to Zeus, or else I will have to take you by force."

Ah, Athena, there is a reason she is called the Goddess of Warfare and Wisdom. She was known as being strategic and not many have won against her and if they did win, she would just kill them later. I wondered what my chances were, even with the helmet of invisibility. Probably low, unless I used my power again, but I had a feeling that would get me into more trouble than it was worth. Well, I didn't know if I could really get into more trouble at this point. Seemed impossible, really.

Melinoe looked at me and smiled. "We got this.

Run."

I was about to say something when she and Pothos let go of my hand and became visible to Athena. Huntley and I had to run before she realized where we stood.

Athena opened her eyes and smiled. "Oh, Melinoe, we meet again."

"Athena, still suffering from those nightmares I gave you all those years ago? Of the man you fell in love with?"

Her lips tightened, but she held her composure. I could only imagine what Melinoe must have done to her. And why exactly had she messed with the Goddess of Wisdom in first place? I mean, she didn't seem like someone you wanted to cross.

"I have never fallen in love with a man, god or human, and you know that."

Pothos coughed. "Liar."

The gossip between gods, I swear, was crazy.

Athena shot him a look. "Do not call me such things. I could have you both tried for disobeying Zeus' orders. Now, stand down or I will have to take you both out to achieve my mission."

"Chrys, run before it's too late!" Melinoe shouted.

Still stunned about everything going on, Huntley pulled me away from the duel and towards the boat. It wasn't that far now, just a few more blocks. I was glad I was good with directions because this city was like a maze. Alleyways went every which way, ending abruptly even. It didn't make sense and just pissed me off.

There weren't that many people out now, not that they could see us, anyway. They simply heard our footsteps, looked, saw nothing, and probably dismissed it as their imagination or ghosts. I heard that there were a lot of ghosts in these parts.

As we were rounding the last corner, almost free of all that was going on, Athena appeared in front of us. Apparently Pothos and Melinoe couldn't handle it. *We were so close.*

"Give up now. It's no use."

She still couldn't see us, but somehow she could sense us, and was able to tell where we stood. She pointed her spear straight at us. "If you do not back down, I will kill this human and his soul will be thrown into Tartarus where they all belong."

I couldn't let that happen and I knew I wouldn't be able to go up against her without Huntley getting in the way or getting hurt. I thought hard about it, whether it was possible to win, whether the rest was worth it.

It wasn't. The sound of Zeus and my father fighting had subsided which only meant someone had won and since Father wasn't here now where he knew we would be, it meant that he wasn't successful—that Zeus had him.

"Fine," I said, taking off the helmet. It was the only thing I could do at this point. Give up and hope no one else would get hurt in the process. "I will go with you."

Huntley shook his head. "No, you can't— "

"There's no other choice, no other outcome. Even if I made it to the Underworld, there are a select few who could come after me under Zeus' orders. I would have to hide for the rest of eternity and I don't want that. I must see what Zeus says and try to get him to spare me. It's the only way."

Huntley frowned, but he knew I was right. There was no other way out of this. I had to plea with Zeus himself for my life.

Chapter 24

Huntley

So… Athena was pretty hot.

I mean, she wasn't Chrys, but yeah, I could see why she was the Goddess of Wisdom and Warfare. She didn't seem like someone you could easily beat in a fight, as she seemed very strategic. Pothos and Melinoe were nowhere to be seen, of which I hoped they were okay. Hell, Athena knew where we were, and we were *invisible*.

From what Chrys had told me months before, she was a virgin goddess who was smarter than most other gods. Virgin, well, I found that a little hard to believe after everything that had happened tonight. Melanie and Pothos were talking about some guy and it didn't seem like any of the gods could be virgins. Didn't blame them, they had a lot of time to kill. I mean, *a lot*.

I wondered what Melinoe meant when she said she haunted Athena with nightmares of the man she loved. And why would she even do that in the first place? I didn't really want to get involved, though; I was just a bit curious. I thought about asking, but after everything I had seen tonight, I had finally learned to keep my mouth shut. There's a first time for everything, am I right?

Prometheus must have really feared Zeus. He was gone in a flash. So was A.J., but I understood why he fled the scene. Hades would have sent him to Tartarus in a heartbeat if he knew he betrayed his daughter like that. But Prometheus, I had no idea why he would turn his back on Chrys. Though, it wasn't like he knew her well enough to really have to stay. It was just odd that he would stand up to

Poseidon, but not to Zeus. And we really needed him back there, or against Athena. Maybe he could have given us a little more time.

I hoped Hades had actually defeated Zeus and that we could all just go home. I knew that probably wasn't the case, that if he had won, he would have been here right now. It was quiet now, the battle already over.

I had never been so afraid in my life, this silence making it all the worse. Chrys was walking straight to her death, if I wasn't mistaken. There was no way she could talk Zeus into letting her live, was there? What could she do to make him change his mind?

Athena led us to the Globe Theatre. Never in my wildest dreams (or highest of highs) did I imagine that I would be trespassing on the property that once held Shakespearian plays hundreds of years ago with a bunch of Greek gods practically involving themselves in a fight to the death. My imagination was never that great though, and now I was living a life, or death, that I never expected.

I peered around as Athena forced us through the

modern lobby and down towards the historic theater replica. Why we were coming here of all places, I had no idea. Because the gods simply could? Probably, I knew I would break into places if I were a god just because I could, making humans not remember I was ever there just as Chrys did at the school. It just wasn't fair, really. that they had this power. I supposed that if they were responsible for all of creation, that they were privy to all sorts of benefits.

Chrys hadn't said a word as Athena escorted us. She had a lot to think about, especially after her father looked at her the way he did. She was probably devastated bringing him all of this drama, though I knew he would do anything for his daughter. But he was still pretty pissed she went behind his back.

I just hoped we all would get out of this okay. That we could return to the pleasant glory days of playing poker, or days spent in Chrys' company without having to worry for her safety all the time. Though that outcome didn't seem likely. Did Greek

Mythology have genies? Maybe we could find a magical lamp and make all this go away.

I mean, what would happen if everything didn't go okay? Would we all be thrown into Tartarus? And what kind of war would Hades and Zeus start? There is a lot that was still up in the air and I didn't have a good grasp on any of it.

We went to the main theater area to find Zeus standing in the middle of the stage. Center of attention, of course. He was still as lively as ever, gold practically radiating off of him. Although he mostly appeared to be okay, I could tell that the fight with Hades had indeed exhausted him. If Chrys could use her powers fully, I was sure she could win against him.

Well... maybe. I liked to think so, but reality was that he was the god of gods, the "big man." Who knew, really, maybe she would win if she had practiced with her powers some more. They were sporadic and untrained now. With some control, she'd be one hell of a fighter. Problem was they were dangerous too, so Hades probably didn't want her practicing much around him. Mostly in fear that she would destroy everything.

Poseidon was there as well, scowling at Chrys as she walked ahead of me. I wondered how much pain she had caused him. Melinoe said she was killing him and bringing him back to life again and again. I could only imagine what that had to feel like, especially to a god. Did it have any lasting damage, particularly psychological damage? That kind of quick alternating between a state of life and death had to have the ability to drive anyone insane.

Though he deserved it. He tried to kidnap her, the daughter of Hades. Did he really think she wasn't going to put up a fight? Not to mention she was his niece, God I needed to stop thinking about their over-complicated family tree. It was sick.

There was no trace of Melinoe or Pothos. I hoped that they were okay, as they had been defeated by Athena. I doubt that she would have completely destroyed them, but as to where they went I had no clue. I hoped one day I could thank them for trying to help us. They really didn't need to.

As we went down the stairs, I noticed there was another person on the side of the stage. I couldn't believe my eyes as I saw a man, bent down on his knees, breathing heavily. He looked weak, tired, unable to fight anymore.

Hades had been defeated.

Chapter 25

Chrys

"Father!" I hurried to his side. Burn marks covered his clothes. He looked up at me, sadness still filling his eyes. He placed a hand on my shoulder.

"I'm fine. Don't worry about me. We will figure out a way out of this, okay?"

I could feel tears wanting to fall out of my eyes, but I wouldn't let them. I would stay strong. I was the daughter of Hades, I could do anything. I wouldn't let anyone defeat me without a fight. Not even Zeus.

I helped Father up, and he glared at Zeus, shaking his head. "You are not taking away my daughter. You don't have the right—"

"I don't?" Zeus snapped. "As if someone like you could have any understanding of what it's like to make sure there's peace and order throughout the universe. No, you only deal with death, with the souls of people who have lived in my world. You have no idea what it is like to have to watch over so many lives, so many parts of nature."

Father snarled, "it is because of you two that I was sent there! It was because neither of you wanted the world that I live in, a world that is dark, a world that had made me bitter. So many years I loathed being there, so many years I pleaded with you to let me have domain of another place. Then I met Persephone, a goddess you promised me, and what did you do? You let her leave. You let her mother persuade you into granting her leave of me even though you promised her to me. Now I have a daughter, a daughter I adore, my one and only flower. I will not let you take her away from me like you took everything else from me!"

Now, I had seen Father angry, but this was beyond just simple anger. This was resentment, a result of pent up anger festering for thousands of years. I knew my father never wanted the Underworld, that he had been tricked into having it, but what he said about Mother was a surprise. He blamed Zeus for her being unfaithful. That was why he never grew angry at her, because he never saw it as being her fault. I wondered what she was like when they first met, if she did love him and what life could have been like if she could never leave the Underworld. Would she have still snuck men in and out? Father probably didn't think so.

And it explained why he cared so much about me, never letting me out of his domain. He had suffered so much and he thought I was his only reward in such a bleak world. I never realized that he felt that I was the only thing he had.

"Such a sad, pathetic story, brother. You feel that your fate is unjust, fine. But don't blame me for your misfortune, for having an unfaithful wife. But you know as well as I do that your daughter will only bring destruction on the worlds that we have fought so hard to protect, or do you not remember? When we fought against the titans together, against our father? The power inside of her could be one that would make that war seem easy if she wanted to fight."

"But I don't want to fight!" I exclaimed. I didn't understand why that was so hard to get through his thick skull. "I just want to live my life in the Underworld! Why can't you see that? Why can't you acknowledge the fact that not everyone wants your spot in Olympus? That some of us just want to live our lives?"

Zeus shook his head. "Is that so? Then how do you explain attacking Poseidon?"

"He attacked us!" I shouted. "He tried to drag me into the ocean itself. If I didn't do anything, he would have kidnapped me!"

Hades shot Poseidon a look, growling, "is that true?"

Poseidon didn't say a word as my father glared at

him. If he was stronger, Father probably would have punched him. Before either of them said anything, Zeus went on. "Even so, you killed him and brought him back to life again and again. That is not something I can look away from. That kind of power is too great for any one god."

"I don't want this power," I said. Honestly, I didn't. It had brought me so much pain and chaos. "But it was given to me by fate. Can't you see that? How can you kill me because of fate? Because of something in the universe declaring that I be born? You say my birth shouldn't have been possible, that my father shouldn't have been able to conceive a child. Don't you think it's a miracle that I was born, that my fate isn't one for you to decide, but the universe itself? How can you claim to be the God of Order and Nature when you don't let nature run its course? That anyone you find threatening you destroy before it becomes too powerful? You aren't following order or nature, you are just making sure that nothing can hurt you."

Zeus stepped towards me, his face inches from

mine. Father tried to protest, but Poseidon grabbed him. My father was still too weak to fight back. But I stood tall. There was no way I was backing down now.

"Do you know what it was like to watch your brothers and sisters be swallowed up by the titan that was my father?" Zeus whispered. "What it was like to have to grow up, hidden from him, increasing my strength so that I would one day be able to defeat them and save my siblings. With help I was able to defeat Cronus and make him regurgitate my family, including your father. Then we went on a long war against all the titans, of which we barely won. So pardon me if I am a little wary of beings who could potentially destroy everything I fought so hard to protect."

I didn't know what to say to that. He did have a point, how hard he had worked to get the world to where it was now, he had every right to worry, but I also had the right to stand up for myself and prove that I wasn't a threat, that I was just a girl who wanted to survive and to return home. I wasn't part of some prophecy, I was just a girl whose fate was still unknown.

"But didn't your father do the same as you did? Destroying Uranus and then becoming paranoid that the world he had created would be overruled by his offspring? Getting rid of them just as you are threatening to get rid of me?" I asked. I knew I had a point, and I had to stick to it. It was my only chance. I knew everyone hated it when you compared them to their parents, just like when someone said I looked like Persephone.

Zeus let a small smile creep onto his lips. "Touché. But I still have to do something with you, I can't just let you walk freely."

I shook my head. "Well I'm not going to die, not without a fight."

Looking me up and down, he studied me. He was probably looking for some kind of weakness, and I wouldn't allow him the satisfaction. I stood tall, not backing down from this fight. His eyes finally stopped scanning me and held my gaze. "I suppose you aren't. Well then, there's only one thing I can do then."

"Oh," I asked. "And what's that?"

"For me to take you as my wife."

Chapter 26

Huntley

My heart practically felt as if it were going to jump out of my chest. There was no way in hell I would let her be with Zeus. Marriage? *Seriously*? What was with these gods? Either death or sex. What was this, the medieval ages? For immortals, this whole marriage thing to make deals or polish things over felt like an out-of-place custom, especially since mortals themselves have moved past it. Why are they still fixated on it? Not to mention, wasn't Zeus technically her grandfather and uncle and had a kid with her mom? I tried not to think about it, as it was all so headache-inducing to think any further. As Chrys had pointed out earlier, family was a very loose term when it came to the gods. The more I thought about it though, the more it made me sick.

Hades started shaking his head, apparently as horrified at the proposal as I was. At least someone still had a brain left. Too bad it was only the God of Death. "No. No. No! I won't allow it! You can't have her. I would never let her marry the likes of you!"

Zeus turned to Hades. "Pick, brother. Would you rather her reside in Tartarus for an eternity or would you rather her reside with me in Olympus?"

Hades looked like it was a hard decision to make. And it was because both were shitty choices. Why couldn't there ever be a good choice in life? "I don't — " He looked at Chrys with such kind eyes. If only she would open his heart and see how much Hades cared about her. Or he did see and simply didn't care. Probably the latter. "I don't want to lose my daughter either way. You know that taking her away from me is just as painful. I need her at my side, I can't go on without my daughter."

"Then you should have taken better watch of her."

Such a dick. All the gods and demigods were dicks. And humans, if we were honest. Why couldn't people just be kind to one another. No, they had to be stubborn, had to have their way. I wished people would care for once about how their action affected others.

Hades shook his head. "No, you know this is wrong. You have had countless women over the years, I have only had one. And have been blessed with a daughter that is my treasure. And you already have a wife! What about Hera? Is she not your wife in Olympus?"

Zeus let out a sigh. "You know how it is with wives, over so many years they start becoming distant and not as interested. I'm sure you know what I mean, how the little things can strain a marriage."

Wow, low blow. Hades didn't say a word, but I could tell he was pissed at what Zeus had said. Hell,

I would have punched him for that comment. After the problems Persephone had caused, the one thing that had kept him going had been his daughter, and now Zeus was trying to take away that as well. Not to mention Zeus slept with almost everyone. He wouldn't be faithful to Chrys and she would end up in the same kind of relationship as her father was in. Except this one never had love in it to begin with.

"I accept," Chrys whispered. Time felt as if it had stopped, as the theater had become silent. Hades and I just stared at Chrys, dumbfounded by her decision. I couldn't believe that she would agree, after everything that had happened. *Was she stupid?* Did she even stop to think about the stomach-wrenching things he would probably do to her? I doubt he would care about her feelings, that was apparent based on his arrogant demonstration. She needed someone who would listen, someone who would do anything for her, not a selfish blowhard like Zeus.

Someone like me.

Hades started shaking his head. "No, no you

can't. I won't allow it."

"She has made up her mind, accept it." Zeus stepped forward, appearing as if he was about to kiss her when Chrys held up her hand.

"With a few conditions," she added. *Good girl.*

Zeus shook his head, not believing that she would do such a thing. "You aren't in a position to ask for conditions."

"They aren't large and won't cause you any trouble. So hear them, will you?" Chrys was getting stronger, bolder, I could see it. She knew she had to stand her ground to survive at this point.

"Fine. What are they?"

"First, I will stay with my father until the wedding, which will be on the next autumn equinox. Second, I will only stay with you from autumn equinox to winter solstice. Three months of the year, just as my mother does for my father. The rest of the time I am in the Underworld. Lastly, you give Huntley immortality and eternal youth just as you did A.J."

Zeus rubbed the scruff on his face, thinking about

this proposal. I wanted to protest that she should add the bit about me, but Zeus went on. "Three months, eh?"

"Why, do you have a problem with that set up? You didn't seem to when you made it for my father."

"Fine. But I can't give your human immortality. He has eaten food in the Underworld, tying him to the place for all of eternity. I can grant him eternal youth, though, and he must die of another cause instead of growing old."

I shook my head. "Wait, I never wanted—"

"Then it's agreed," Chrys interrupted.

Zeus grabbed her and kissed her hard, giving Hades a look of triumph as he did so. I thought Hades had been furious before the proposal, now I could see the fire burn in his eyes. I could see how much hate he had for his brother, for the man who had taken his daughter away from him.

And I felt exactly the same.

I couldn't imagine this monster having his hands on my Chrys, on the girl I had grown to love with all my heart. She didn't deserve this, she didn't deserve any of this. And then to try to get me not to return to the Underworld, I didn't understand. I didn't want that, I didn't like it on Earth. I just wanted to be in the Underworld with her.

But there was nothing I could say at this point. She had made up her mind. I had to go along with it, at least for now.

Zeus backed away from Chrys, finally, smiling in triumph. "Well then, in eleven months time we shall wed. Hades, you can take her back home and get her ready."

Hades didn't say another word as Poseidon let him go. He walked over to Chrys. "Come on, let's go."

I could see the upset in her eyes as he didn't try to comfort her, simply was disappointed in everything that had happened. She knew that due to her own error, all of this had transpired. She had to accept that.

But I wouldn't.

Chapter 27

Chrys

I stood out on the patio, staring out at the souls that showered down into Tartarus. I would have been one of those people if it hadn't been for Zeus proposing, giving me a way to cheat death, at least for a while. Who knew, maybe I would end up hating him so much I would just kill myself. No, I wouldn't do that to my father, not after everything that had transpired.

I wished that there had been another way out of this, that I could have been stronger to defeat him.

Maybe if I hadn't had to fight Poseidon before he showed up, I would have been alright. Maybe I did have enough power to fight him.

Who was I kidding? I wished that I had never disobeyed my father.

I hadn't seen Father for the past couple of days since we got back to the Underworld. I presumed he told Persephone what had happened. I had heard them fighting every night since we came back. They had never fought this much before. Perhaps Father blamed Mother for leaving out the rings, or how she was being such an uncaring mother, causing me to run. Either way, I knew I couldn't blame her. This was my doing and mine alone.

The worst part of it all? There was no one to come knocking on my door, bringing me some pomegranate seeds, turning up the music for me. No one to hold me as I wept through the night. There was no more Huntley.

I looked down at the friendship bracelet, the one thing I would never get rid of, the one thing I had to remind me of him. I had left him on Earth, making

Zeus give him eternal youth. I knew, even though it would have been just for a little bit of time, that he would try to stop me from marrying Zeus if he was in the Underworld. If Zeus somehow found out, he would have Huntley chained up somewhere immediately. I couldn't let that happen, I couldn't let him be in harm's way more than he already had been.

I wished that I could have properly said goodbye, to tell him that I would miss him, that although we had only known each other for a short time, that I had loved him and cared for him with every fiber of my being. He had become a large part of my life, and I wanted anything other than to let him go. It hurt, almost as much as my father's disappointment in me. And the fact A.J. had betrayed me so easily. If I ever see that two-faced bastard's face again...

I heard the door open behind me. I turned to find my father standing there. He still had that far-off gaze, but at least he had finally come to see me. I had wanted to talk to him for so long, I could barely sleep, even if I needed to.

"Father…" I began.

"Chrys. What are you doing out here?" he asked. He still didn't appear to want to talk. It felt like a blade had stabbed me in the chest.

I glanced out at Tartarus. There were so many going down there lately. Why had I never noticed that before since returning? "I'm just thinking about everything."

"About how you disobeyed me?"

I didn't like how he said the word 'disobeyed'. I was in enough agony, I didn't need to be reminded. "I didn't think— "

"That's right, you didn't think. Why did you even leave? You knew the risk."

"I didn't think that just a few days would be a problem," I whispered.

Father rubbed his temples. He was beyond stressed now. I had never seen him like this before. I wanted to help, but I knew there was nothing I could do at this point. I had really screwed things up.

He looked out at the Underworld. "Yeah, well,

you were wrong weren't you?"

"I'm sorry, I really am…"

"Now Zeus will have you and I am alone again. All of what I have done since you have been born has been for your safety. And now he has you."

"But I will be here when Mother is away, I made sure that was part of the agreement for you."

He turned to face me. "You don't understand, Chrys, I can't stand thinking of what he will do to you. The three months that you are with him, how you are my daughter, the brother he likes to hurt, the brother he likes to cause pain. Now he has you and I can't even comprehend what…" Hades closed his eyes. "You have any idea how many women he has been with? He tricked your mother long ago, as you probably know since I saw Melinoe with you. He has destroyed countless lives, and above everything he has always wanted to push me down. I have let him all this time, knowing he could never touch what was important to me. He couldn't touch you. Now he can, and I don't know what to do."

"Father I'm so sorry. I just wanted to know what it

was like out there. I'm sorry, I really am."

"It's too late for apologies, my flower. Now you will belong to him, and everything will have been for nothing. All because you wanted to see the world." He placed his hand on my shoulder and stared in my eyes. Great sadness filled them, sadness that had taken root even before I was born. "Just tell me, was it worth it?"

With that, he turned back to the palace and went inside. Tears streamed down my face. I had lost everything because of one choice. A choice I should have never made.

Chapter 28

Huntley

"We have to do something. We have to stop this." I paced back and forth in Pothos' house, trying to comprehend still all that had happened. Chrys had been taken to the Underworld, getting ready to marry Zeus. It had happened so fast, I just wanted it all to go back to how it was.

Melinoe and Pothos sat together on the couch, watching as I walked all around. Melinoe kept shaking her head. "There isn't anything we can do. It's Zeus, it isn't like we can go against him, stop him, or even kill him. There is nothing we can do."

I hated hearing that, that there was nothing we could do. Of course there had to be *something* we could do, and I wasn't going to go down without a fight. This was Chrys, I owed everything to her. She had fished me out of the rivers of the Underworld, gave me compassion and love. And now, here I was, stuck on Earth, unable to console her. I thought about jumping off a bridge, or in front of a bus, but the fact that could just leave me floating in a river, never to be found, it didn't seem like it could help. By the time someone found me, centuries could have passed and Chrys will have suffered so much.

So I had to figure out how to stop the wedding without going to the Underworld. And that's what led me to be at Pothos' house.

I found them after the others left for their respected domains. I was just standing there, alone, like a sad little puppy. They dragged me, kicking and screaming, as I tried to jump in the River Thames. They are the ones who pointed out that if I drowned, then I couldn't help Chrys. Stupid people and their well thought out ideas. So now we sat here, trying to figure out a plan we could instigate to stop this wedding that would happen in eleven months.

"But there has to be a way to get her out of this marriage," I said as I looked down at my friendship bracelet. Every moment I saw it it reminded me of her. "A way to get Zeus to call it off."

Pothos stood up, biting his lip, a finger extended as if he had an idea. "There's only one person who would be able to help us, one of the few people who has gone up against him and survived. We would have to find him, get him to help us. It won't be easy, though, as he has great reason to fear Zeus."

I shook my head. "Who then?"

"That…" A voice started and as I turned, I found Prometheus standing there. He looked nervous, just as before. He held his hat in his hands, squeezing it. "Would be me."

Thank You For Reading!

Thank you so much for reading! Readers like you make it possible for authors like me to write stories! If you could spare a moment and leave a review on Amazon, Goodreads, BookBub, and wherever you like to buy books, that would mean the world to me! It really helps authors like me to succeed in the publishing world.

A big thank you again for your patronage. I hope you will check out the next book in the series and my other series. Keep reading to get a sneak peak of Book 2 of Daughter of Hades: Engaged!

CHAPTER 1

Chrys

I lay there in my bed, listening to *Hanging On* by Falling in Reverse. I could stay here forever, let time waste away until the wedding. I could just stare up at the posters I had of different bands I liked—the bands that Huntley had introduced me to.

Placing my arm over my eyes, I tried to push back the

tears. I was stronger than this, I knew, but damn it still hurt to realize how much I lost in such a short time frame. For hundreds of years I was living down here in the Underworld, never really caring about what happened on the surface. Then finally I snapped at Persephone and I just had to know.

What was up there that was so damn important?

I knew I really shouldn't blame her as this was all my fault. It was my decision to go to Earth and disobey Father's direct orders. I should have listened to him, and I should have listened to Huntley. He knew it was a bad idea from the start, but he stayed by my side to make sure I remained safe.

And now Huntley was gone.

The realization that I wouldn't ever see him again came back to me and the tears made their way down the sides of my face. Damn it, I shouldn't have started to think about it all again. This was literally torture.

No, what was to come would be torture.

Because of my mistake, because I was a fool who didn't listen to what her father said, I would have to marry Zeus, a god who wanted to see my destruction and wanted to watch my father suffer. On top of that, he was known for his affairs, his illegitimate (and legitimate) children, and just causing a lot of trouble all around. He was the God of Gods, Ruler of Olympus, and he got to do pretty much whatever he wanted, and my short time on Earth definitely taught me that. I had stepped into the big family drama, how lucky was I?

Now Father wasn't speaking to me, and I doubted I would win his trust back. I had always thought he was overprotective, just thinking that something horrible would happen because he worried too much. Apparently I was wrong, since something did in fact happen.

And it threw my entire world into the gutter. Between Huntley being gone, having AJ betray me after hundreds of years of friendship, and Father giving me the cold shoulder, none of my life would ever be back to normal. Then, in a few months, I would be married to Zeus and... I didn't even want to think of what would h*appen next.*

*Baby, I adore you, but this ain't gonna la*st forever.

I rubbed my face dry and got up out of my bed. It was still morning at least, but probably a lot later than when I should have gotten up. I theoretically was supposed to help Father with judging since Persephone was gone, although he hadn't been too strict about it lately. It was my duty, though, I would be there when she was away, condemning souls with Father. At least I would never have to see Persephone's face again. I wondered if she even cared.

Father wasn't too happy about how much Persephone pushed me into leaving. Although I didn't blame her after everything that had happened, knowing it was my own selfish desire that led me to Earth, Father hadn't come to that conclusion yet. He blamed her for most of it. It was because of her magical rings we had used to travel between worlds, it was her dragging men down here, talking constantly about how much she hated it here that made him lose his daughter. At least, that's what I heard him yell at her on more than one occasion. There were countless nights where they kept me awake crying under the covers as they argued just as she left. I hadn't seen him this mad at her since, well, ever. However, I've seen Mother mad at Father many times over. So I guess it was only fair.

Changing into some simple black clothes, skinny jeans, a tank, and boots, I threw my hair back and stared at myself in the mirror. I finally understood why my father always wore black, it definitely fit the mood lately. Although we sometimes could stand being in the same room with each other, that didn't mean he really spoke to me, at least not like he used to. So it felt darker here than it ever did before. Gods could hold grudges and I wasn't looking forward to how long this atmosphere was going to last.

Deciding to grab some breakfast, I strolled down the hallways, taking my time since I didn't necessarily want to help judge souls at that moment. The entire castle was pretty quiet, especially after everything that had happened. I had always grown up thinking they were so silent, but now with everyone gone and being somewhat neglected by Hades, I now knew what real silence was like. And it sucked.

I still had my puppy Cerberus at least, and spoiled him rotten. If he weren't with Father right now, he would be following me around, wanting to play. I had gathered some bones for him last night and couldn't wait to watch as his many heads fought over who got to chew the bone first.

I could tell he missed Huntley, as he liked to mess with the human. Most people were automatically afraid of him, and Huntley at first was pretty terrified. But he started to warm up to Cerberus, and Cerberus took advantage of that. At least injuries here healed pretty quickly, as everyone here was already dead.

So right now I was alone. After all these years I thought I was fine with being alone, as there weren't many people who wanted to hang out with the daughter of Hades, but I realized I was wrong. I hadn't known true loneliness until now.

I did get closer with the chef recently, since he prepared my meals and put them aside without Father knowing. Hades didn't like that I had been sleeping in and told the chef to stop making me meals late in the morning. It was really petty of Father, but I did feel bad when the chef got everything back out to make me something. So we decided it would be best to just make me something and put it in the fridge. I could at least reheat it.

The head chef most recently was a man named Vincenzo from a small town in Italy, where apparently the best chefs lived, at least according to Persephone. Then Father gave him the option to stay and be a chef for a few months or so and then he would be able to go to Elysian Fields. Would anyone pass up an offer like that?

Sneaking into the kitchen, trying not to distract any of

the other chefs and Vincenzo as they were preparing lunch. Had I really slept in that long? I checked the clock. Yup, it was almost eleven. Vincenzo glanced over to me and waved with a smile. I waved back and mouthed a 'thank you', especially since he shouldn't have to deal with a lazy goddess like me.

Opening the fridge, I found the plate with some Egg Florentine. It looked delicious. Vincenzo always had the most flavorful of florentines that I had ever had. This one had artichoke, roasted garlic, caramelized onions, and sun-dried tomatoes.

I swiftly put it in the oven and let it heat as I fumbled around with the tea kettle. Ever since I went to England, I had been craving Earl Grey tea. I liked having it every morning as it woke me up completely and gave me just enough energy to get through the day without giving me the jitters. Just as the kettle was done and the tea had steeped, the Florentine was ready to go. I grabbed it and retreated into the dining hall.

I never understood why the dining hall was so large when there was theoretically only three of us. It was pretty grand too, with scrolls hanging on the wall, mainly weaved landscapes of the Underworld. Mother always hated them and sometimes threw drinks at them when she was angry. As for the table, it was a long, dark wood with a dark grey table liner. It could sit probably fifty people at this table, if not more. For centuries we have never had guests down here.

It suddenly hit me—was it because no one could find

out I existed? Did Father have more people visiting before I was born? Was I the reason he was alone here?

I don't know why it never occurred to me before now, with all this grandeur that encompassed the castle, that maybe it was for guests besides the deceased. Maybe Father gave all that up just for me. And that was why me leaving made him feel so much more betrayed than just a simple disobedient act.

Sitting down, I clapped my hands together and said,"thank you for the meal!" and dug straight in. There was no point in thinking about what life was like before I was around anymore—especially since now he could go back to that lifestyle, as the secret of my existence was out in the open.

I figured I would have the dining hall alone for a while, especially since it was between meals, but as I was halfway through my breakfast, the door to the main hallway opened. I glanced up to find Hades standing there. I jumped up out of my chair, almost choking on my food in the process. I coughed, trying to get it back up or force it down.

"Did I startle you?" he asked with almost no hint of emotion. It was the same tone he had every time he talked to me. It was worse than when he didn't talk to me. I couldn't tell what kind of things he was thinking when he spoke like that. Was it hatred? Resentment? Frustration? I didn't know and had a feeling I would never find out.

I nodded. "Yeah, I figured you would be working." Which was the truth, as that was all he did most of the day. Even though that was his job in the Underworld, it felt like he had been working more than normal lately.

"I was working, and you were supposed to be too, or have you forgotten your duties?"

I finally got the peace of artichoke down and coughed once more to clear anything else in my throat. "Yeah, well, I woke up late."

"And so you figured you would just skip out on the whole day?"

Shrugging, I didn't answer his question. Yeah, I had been hoping I could skip especially since he had been giving me the cold shoulder as I sat there and watched the Three Stooges, the three judges that helped him with handling all the dead. I liked calling them that because they weren't the sharpest knives in the light sockets sometimes. They had been assigned by Zeus to make sure Hades was doing his job, as if he wasn't trustworthy. I guess when you were a lying piece of shit god, you just expected all the other gods to be the same.

Father ended the awkward silence between us. "Well, I need you to help me."

"Can I finish eating at least?" I asked, gesturing to the meal I was in the middle of eating.

He glanced to my plate of food. "What did I tell you about making Vincenzo cook you something so late in the morning?"

Damn it, he remembered. "He didn't, he just leaves leftovers and I reheat it."

"And what did I tell you about reheating a chef's

food?"

I sighed. "That it's rude and I should wake up on time when it's fresh."

"Exactly. We will discuss this later. Now hurry up."

Hades stood there, not leaving the room like I expected him to.

"Are… are you waiting here for me?" I asked.

"Yes, now hurry it up."

I quickly downed the rest of my food, which I thought was more disrespectful to Vincenzo than reheating it, but that wasn't going to be a conversation Father and I would be having. If I tried to point out any of his faults lately, I got my head bitten off. It was better to just to not say anything.

BUY ENGAGED *ONLINE OR AT YOUR LOCAL BOOKSTORE*

Acknowledgments

I want to thank everyone who made this novel possible. A big thank you to my editor Justin Boyer who hopefully hasn't gotten sick of reading my stories yet. Thank you to Biserka Design for the amazing covers for this series! I love them lot! A special thank you to Dr. Almira Poudrier at ASU for answering my questions about Greek Mythology as things get weird and confusing and even more weird. And, lastly, thank you to my husband and parents who are always supporting me.

About the Author

Dani Hoots is a science fiction, fantasy, romance, and young adult author who loves anything with a story. She has a B.S. in Anthropology, a Masters of Urban and Environmental Planning, a Certificate in Novel Writing from Arizona State University, and a BS in Herbal Science from Bastyr University.

Currently she is working on a YA urban fantasy series called Daughter of Hades, a YA urban fantasy series called The Wonderland Chronicles, a historic fantasy vampire series called A World of Vampires, and a YA sci-fi series called Sanshlian Series. She has also started up an indie publishing company called FoxTales Press. She also works with Anthill Studios in creating comics through Antik Comics.

Her hobbies include reading, watching anime, cooking, studying different languages, wire walking, hula hoop, and working with plants. She is also an herbalist and sells her concoctions on FoxCraft Apothecary. She lives in Phoenix with her husband and visits Seattle often.

Feel free to email her with any questions you might have!
danihootsauthor@gmail.com

Made in the USA
Las Vegas, NV
17 May 2021

23177132R00187